Devil's Playgrou[

Desire

Trigger warning,

This book series contains content that might be troubling for some readers. This includes but not limited to adult content, sexual activities, various kink and fetishes, rape, substance abuse, substance use, death, suicide, nightmares/night terrors, PTSD, various trauma, profanity, and so on.

Each chapter has the possible trigger warnings under the title. Please take care of your mental health when reading Devil's Playground book series.

Devil's

Playground

Desire

Chapters

Welcome,

My name is Kendra, a single successful lawyer here in Las Vegas, Nevada. If you are new here, be a good little reader and pick up the first book of the trilogy Devil's Playground Toxicity to understand how I got here in my journey. Then come back and spread my pages.

If you have already read that book. Welcome back home my good little reader. It looks like someone is addicted. Now, could it be because my life is a chaotic mess or are you just into the sex? My thoughts are going with you are into the sex. Nothing wrong with that. We all need a good release.

Now back to business, as the plot thickens in my life. The rollercoaster of drama is just the tip of the iceberg that will also have your lips tingling. Which lips? Well, I guess you are going to have to read to find out.

So, buckle up.

Kendra

Chapter 1
Interrogation

This chapter contains:
Profanity

I was used to putting people in the back of cop cars, being in the back of one feels surreal. We made our way through the city to get to the station. My hands were in cuffs behind my back, as much as I fought tears, I could not help it. I used my shoulder to wipe the tears on my face. I glanced towards the front, I could see the officers cracking jokes and smiling though the glass that separated us. Finally, we got to the station, and I was immediately taken into the interrogation room my mind was frantically rushing through the events that led up to Mr. Dupont's death.

All I could think about was the fact I was innocent, we were having consensual sex and while my back was turned from him, he stopped breathing, then his hand dropped. I started having a panic attack. The thought of having necrophilia made me nauseous to my stomach. My heart was racing a thousand miles an hour and my breathing was getting shallow. Raising my arms above my head I gasped for air. I ran my fingers through my hair as I sat on the metal chair awaiting my fate. I tried to calm myself down with the techniques that my therapist gave me. I waited as patiently as I could for Detective Kilian to come in and interrogate me. It felt like an eternity waiting for them to arrive to determine my fate.

The door opened and in stepped a tall, buff, handsome, tanned man with black graduation hair style with matching black eyes. He was dressed in slacks and a company polo shirt. His deep voice calmed my nerves. *"Ms. Kendra, I am Detective Killian, nice to meet you, can you tell me what happened this evening."* I sighed before answering *"Hi Detective Killian, unfortunately we do have to meet this way.*

Mr. Dupont and I had an evening celebrating my victory in court earlier yesterday. As the evening went on acts between two consenting adults took place. In the middle of said acts with my back turned is when everything went south."
Detective Killian adjusted himself and started to go hardball *"Kendra, let's be honest, you put something in his drink."* I interrupted him immediately *"If you are going to put blame on me that never happened, I will call my lawyer and stop talking, you can dust his glass and whiskey decanter my fingerprints are nowhere on them besides my glass."* Before he could speak there was a knock on the door. Officer Riggs comes bursting into the room with the Coroner Jasmine. Mr. Dupont died of an aneurysm.

They put in a copy of the DVD from the security cameras showing our evening from when we entered his house, to the drinks we shared, music we played, and even the bedroom activities. I knew that old man was a pervert, but I had no clue he had a thing for voyeurism. My face blushed when it got to our bedroom scene. I had no idea that I was being recorded. I looked towards Detective Killian with innocent eyes I noticed he was fixing his stance, was Detective Killian getting turned on from watching our act? Coroner Jasmine explained that *"Mr. Dupont had a brain aneurysm that killed him instantly during our activities and that more than likely he did not experience any symptoms, it was fast and painless."* Weakness flooded my body as my innocence was proven tonight.

After several hours, I was signing documents to regain my freedom with Detective Killian. I was hesitant to speak with him because I was exhausted, but I also didn't want to risk incriminating myself with simple flirting, especially since he just watched me ride a dead corpse. I do have to say this, Detective Killian had an intoxicating cologne. As he leaned in to show me where to sign, all I could do was inhale his aroma of apple, oak, cedar, labdanum, and vanilla. I watched his hands closely and I could see his veins go all way the way up his arm. All I could think to myself was how sexy his arms must look pinning me down. I stayed professional because I did not want a sexual harassment charge for hitting on the detective who almost had me behind bars for a death I did not do.

I slipped him my business card and in a seductive whisper *"You can email me the copies or bring them down to my office when you get a chance."* He nodded his head confirming that he got the hint of where I was going with this. I was too tired to read into his actions. Trying to figure out how to get back to my car I asked Detective Killian if he or his officer could give me a ride back to my vehicle so I could get home safely. Detective Killian answered *"You are too exhausted to drive home, I will take you home myself. My officers will bring your vehicle home before morning. You are not in a safe state to drive yourself home."* I softly grinned at his orders *"Yes sir."* He fought his smile when I said that. We made our way to his city issued car, Detective Killian was a gentleman and reached for the passenger door. The veins on his arm sent chills down my body. I sat down and looked up towards him *"Thank you"*. He coughed and cleared his throat; I think he was catching on to my game. *"You're welcome, Kendra."*

He was quiet during the ride home. I fought my hardest to stay awake. It was a challenge because I was drifting off while Detective Killian drove in silence. We made it back to the house in twenty minutes. Shockingly, Detective Killian got out and walked with me to my front door. He put his arm on my door frame after I unlocked it. Turning to face him, inches away from him beautiful thick lips, I couldn't help but stare at them. I tried my best to look up into his eyes. But in a low seductive voice *"Get some rest Kendra, I will drop off copies to your office"* my knees buckled *"Of course, can't wait to see you again Detective Killian."* I answered in a flirtatious tone licking my lips. He opened my door to let me inside and winked. I walked inside and locked my door, without making it very far exhaustion flooded my body. I was too weak to walk upstairs. I sat on the couch to take off my shoes, and I instantly crashed on the couch.

7

With a couple hours passing for sleep it was time to wake up to go into the office. I was exhausted from the activities the night before. It will be a long day after only getting 4 hours of sleep. I drank my coffee and slowly got ready. In my head all I could think was fuck I don't have my car. Reaching for my phone to dial for help from Nick. I got a message from an unknown number.

Unknown: Your keys are in the mailbox – Killian

I would be lying if a smile didn't cross my face. So, I answered him back

Kendra: Thank you for leaving them in the mailbox, remember you promised to swing by my office to drop off the copies. Don't forget □

With such an insane night, I am positive that Killian is sleeping peacefully right now. I was rushing to get to work. I grabbed everything and made my way to the office but first I stopped at a coffee shop and grabbed a double shot of espresso.

The day was dragging on, by lunch time I was so exhausted I could not find an appetite to eat. Leaning out of my office door, I said *"Mindy, I am going to take a nap if I am going to last the rest of the day."* She nodded and said, *"I will wake you when lunch is over, sweet dreams."* I closed my office, turned off the light, and shut the blinds. I set my alarm and curled up on the loveseat in my office.

Mindy was so sweet she grabbed a cup of coffee before she came into my office. Ever so sweetly she called out *"Kendra, it's time to wake up. I have a cup of coffee for you. Lunch time is over."* I slowly sat up and stretched, slowly rolling my neck to get the kink out. I answered, *"Thank you Mindy, I appreciate it."* Mindy left the coffee on my desk and opened the blinds to let some light in before turning on the harsh office lights. I rubbed my face, stood up slowly, and took a couple sips of hot coffee. A yawn escaped from my mouth, and I started to walk towards the lights to turn them on. I went back to my desk to check on my emails when someone knocked on the door. Mindy popped her head in *"Someone is here for you, a Detective Killian."* I sprung up and had immediately energy *"Yes, please send him in."* I adjusted myself to look more awake.

Detective Killian walked in *"Hello Kendra, I am doing as you requested."* It was his off day; he wore form-fitting jeans and a plain white t shirt that looked amazing against his tan skin. He handed me a manila folder with the copies of last night's paperwork. I smiled and accepted the folder. *"Thank you, Detective Killian."* My fingers laid upon his as I grabbed the folder, smiling as I accepted the folder. We chatted for a couple of minutes. I hope I was reading the nonverbal cues correctly, because it seemed like sparks were flying between us as we joked and talked like two old crushes.

To my surprise we both tested the water and made a couple of flirtatious remarks to see how far we could push what this was exactly. Harmoniously, we were on the same page taking the next step. He chimed in with a joke *"Since you're not a criminal, do you want to come over for a night swim tonight?"* In my head I was exhausted but at the same time I was really feeling this man and getting to see him soaking wet as a golden-brown God, I could not pass it up. *"Of course,"* I answered. He texted me his address before leaving.

Little did I know that I would have a guest waiting in my office after walking Detective Kilian to the parking lot. Tasha and Nick waited patiently for my return to get the gossip on the hottie who was in my office. Mindy was on a quick break so she could not give me the heads up. When I walked in, I was immediately introduced with interrogating questions of who that handsome stud was, is he single, how do you know each other, and so on.

They asked several rapid-fire questions. I tried my best to answer them as fast as I could until they found out I was partially arrested and taken in for questioning. I explained everything to them, and they could not believe what they were hearing. It has been a long night and it continues when we are swimming in his pool. Their eyes opened wide, and both squealed about how crazy my love life is. I need a tv show with how chaotic it truly is.

When work ended it was time to get ready for my swimming pool date. I won't lie, I am very nervous to go to his house. With the incident that happened, I knew I was innocent but felt like I was still in trouble with everything, like the sensation of walking on thin ice. What is even worse, he already knew how I was in bed from watching the recording. I had no idea what to expect tonight. Looking through my collection of bikinis, I pulled out three bikinis: a glistening red string, a black thong, and a grey snakeskin halter. I decided to play it safe and keep it a little more modest and still a little sexy. I went with my grey snakeskin halter bikini. I paired it with my black cover up skirt and strappy heel sandals.

My stomach was in knots making my way to Detective Killian's house. But I decided to shake it off and stop by the liquor store to bring something for the amazing host. Plus, after I received a group text, I went from being a nervous wreck to laughter.

Nick: Be safe, hoe!

Tasha: Enjoy getting pounded!

I laughed as I made my way out of the car. I took a deep breath and rang Detective Killian's doorbell. He answered after a few seconds, one hand on the door frame, shirtless in swim trunks, his luscious black hair was messy, while every muscle was flexed. In my head I was like yes, pin me inside this door frame and have your way with me. I softly smiled and handed him a bottle of Chateau Megyer Tokaji. *"A gift for having me come over."* He accepted the wine and said, *"My favorite, thank you."*

We stepped out into the backyard, my mouth dropped with how beautiful it was. Certainly, a backyard for entertainment. He had a beautiful outdoor kitchen where Detective Killian was cooking a delicious dinner consisting of steak and grilled vegetables. Our conversations flowed effortlessly, and I couldn't help but get lost staring at his muscles whenever he would focus on cooking. I was behaving and followed his subtle flirting. I tested the water and gently touched his shoulder with my fingers, bumping my hip into his. He smiled and bumped back into me; he did take me by surprise and reached for something behind me pinning me to the counter as he smiled deviously. The tension was building between us. I was not going to complain. I had hundreds of thoughts on how to make this man mine tonight. I don't think he will fight me on it either.

After dinner and an amazing conversation, it was finally time to get wet. Detective Killian jumped in, I tried my best to be seductive and make my way down the steps. I pretended that the water was cold at the knee point. *"It's a little chilly"* I said holding my arms and shivering a bit. Killian smiled and walked up to me and said, *"I will help you warm up."* He grabs me around my waist and pulls me into the water. My arms are draped around his neck, Detective Killian smiles as we are face to face as we both smiled at each other soaking wet. His hands grab my hips.

I decided to surprise him and wrap my legs around his waist. He looked at my lips with a seductive look and back up to my eyes. His hand grabs the back of my head as he kisses me passionately. His held on to my ass cheek and walked us over to a jet and pressed me against it as he pushes himself against my pelvis, biting my lower lip tugging gently. I can feel him getting harder as he grinds himself between each kiss that is exchanged. Detective Killian whispered in my ear *"your snakeskin will look better off of you"* he kisses and nibbles on my neck which sends me into intoxicated trance.

He spins me around to face the water jet slipping off my bottoms and spreading my legs with his, so the jets hit me just right on my clit. I slip off my top to expose my breasts, his large hands scoop up my breast and massage them gently as lips dance across my back with kisses and nibbles. I start to melt from the sensation. As my body weakens with his touch he steps back and removes his swim shorts. We teased each other while we swam to the other side of the pool where the waterfall was. Grabbing each other, pulling one another close, exchanging kisses and teasing each other while rubbing my lips against his shaft.

He lifted me up on the edge under the waterfall where waterfall was pouring on my clit as he buried his tongue deep inside. Quickly I came from the pleasure, screaming "*OH KILLIAN!*" He grabbed my breast as he ate me like a hungry beast. While my body started to convulse, he pulled up and made his way inside my pulsating pussy. Thrusting hard and deep as we locked lips, I could taste my juices from his tongue. Both of us losing control moaning into each other's shoulder.

He slides us back into the pool where a jet was pressing me up against it as he thrust harder into my backside and pulls my hair back letting me know he was in charge. My body starts convulsing uncontrollably as his balls help the jets massage my clit. *"OH GOD YES KILLIAN!"* every time I scream his name it releases a beast inside to go insane inside my pussy. Before it was his turn to cum, he sat on the ledge as I sucked him hard and fucked his cock with my mouth. Deep throating him and massaging his balls so he can unload into my mouth while swallowing every drop as I stare deep into his black eyes. Watching his head roll back in pleasure as I suck up every lost drop.

I crawl up his sexy relaxed body and kiss him softly and whisper in his ear "You taste amazing." He smiled and pulled me on top of him and kissed me softly and holding me close. After several hours of cuddling and enjoying each other's company. He let me borrow his shirt for my ride home. Pressing me against my car and kissing me softly, Killian whispered in my ear *"Don't stay a stranger."* I whispered back *"I won't be."*

Chapter 2

Conference

This chapter contains:

Profanity

At work the next day, I had no clue I would be walking into a meeting with eager horny puppies. Tasha and Nick patiently waited for me to walk into my office to get the juicy details of last night. Before I could get settled in, they were asking nonstop questions. Of course, like a lady I did keep some details private. But both squealed like middle school age girls when I told them he sent me home in one of his shirts to sleep in. I could feel my cheeks turning rosy as I talked about our night and how he didn't want me to be a stranger. Was I getting my hopes up? It would not surprise me with the recent luck I have had with men.

We all separated from our little meeting of last night's rendezvous. I tried to focus on my work when I got a text message from Detective Killian.

Detective Killian: Last night was amazing, have a great day. Xo

I was smiling ear to ear from his sweet text message. So of course, I replied, I also attached a photo of me seductively posing in his shirt in front of my floor length mirror.

Kendra: It was amazing, hope you like the picture.

Detective Killian: Absolutely love it.

My heart was fluttering and my crush for Killian was growing rapidly. Mindy walked in with an envelope addressed to me. I had to sign this for you, it was delivered with urgent material. I took the envelope from her and read it.

Dear Kendra,

As the late Mr. Dupont's attorney, it came to my understanding that he had added you as his concubine before his final breaths. With his wife being deceased, their children have got their share of his will, and due to his policy Mr. Dupont wanted to make sure his partners would be taken of as well. Please contact me to fill out the paperwork to receive you portion of his will.

Harrison Law Attorney,

Bethany Lawson

To my surprise, I could not believe what I was reading, especially since everything happened so quickly. I honestly was not expecting anything from the passing of Mr. Dupont. I wanted to take a couple days to think about it, but unfortunately these usually come with a time frame that must be met. Taking a deep breath, I reached for my office phone to call Mr. Dupont's attorney. We scheduled a meeting to go over what exactly was left for me. I never had anything like this happen to me. I am not sure how I feel about this.

Lunch time rolled around, and the gang went down to the café. I guess my face was giving a concerned look. Because Tasha and Nick were questioning what was going on. If it was trouble in paradise with Detective Killian or something else. I told them about Mr. Dupont putting me in his books as a sugar baby and the surprise letter I received from his lawyer. They were surprised that I even agreed to meet his attorney even though it did not last longer than that night. But what kind of policy did he have to even consider myself special when the agreement started and ended that night.

I made my boss aware that I was going to be late coming in since I had a meeting with Bethany Lawson this morning. Dressed in my impressive suit and my hair curled. I made my way to her office with confidence. I knocked on her door. She answered with a smile *"Good morning, you must be Kendra, ready to go over the documents?"* Surprised at her calm kind energy I stated *"Yes, of course."* I do apologize for the recent loss of Mr. Dupont. I received an email hours before his passing addressing you as his primary special." Bethany mentioned.

Confused by the primary special comment I asked, *"Is there a way you could elaborate on his words."* She cleared her throat *"I have no way of knowing his meaning of primary special, however when he put his policy in place there were rules, we set in place. After Mrs. Dupont died, Mr. Dupont did not want to share his heart with another, he had other sugar partners whom by his policy received a healthy portion of his will after being with him for a while. Because you were assigned and dismissed the same day due his death, he called you his lucky charm with a poker game, he had his eyes set on you for a while and not in a dismissive way. He knew something was good about you and wanted to make sure you were taken care of either way. In his will he granted you $300,000 per his request."* Too stunned to speak after hearing the amount; it felt as if I was in a dream.

Bethany refused to hand me a check due to safety. We walked across the street to the bank and had it wired to my account. The bank teller stated that the money will be in my account within 72 hours. Bethany and I walked back to the office and shook hands in the lobby. We parted ways and I doubt we will ever see each other again. I could not believe that I had $300,000 transferred into my account. What should I do with that money?

I went straight to work after the meeting, with what just happened this morning, I could hardly focus on anything. My mind was rushing about the fact I was three hundred thousand dollars richer. Granted yes as an attorney I do make a good income. However, I never thought I would be given that much cash for basically a one-night stand. I wanted to be smart with this, I was not going to tell a soul about this, I was not sure if I was going to invest or hold it into my savings. I had to think long and hard about this.

I had to get my head right and focus on the work ahead of me. Although my work was minimal, I still wanted to stay ahead of the game. Tasha and Nick rushed into my office telling me I had to come see something. Mindy was turning up the volume on the television. Everyone in the office was silent as we watched Detective Killian inform the news crews and all the citizens of Las Vegas about a horrific quadruple murder with a suspect still on the run. Both Nick and Tasha held onto my hand as the news broke. Hearing Detective Killian give orders about safety and what to watch out for sent shivers down my spine. The suspect is targeting women and apparently there could be more who are murdered with the discrete clues the suspect has given. We just stood there looking at each other. All of us are at risk of danger. More danger than normal that you can get into in the city of sin.

Tasha pulled me aside and asked me to text Detective Killian if it is safe enough to go on outings or if we should hold back and partake in only at home activities. I agreed and quickly sent one out.

Kendra: Hey Killian, question about your statement. Would going out in groups to public settings put us in danger? Should we lay low until a suspect is captured? I am a little scared.

I was not expecting a quick reply because he was talking to the news crew. Everyone in the office slowly got back to work after the horrific news. An hour later, Detective Killian answered me back.

Detective Killian: If anything happens to you, my heart will shatter. Professionally, lay low. Personally, be safe and be hyperaware.

After reading that text message I slumped into my chair. Before walking to Tasha and Nick's office. I am confused by his text message, but I also think the message is loud and clear. With confusion on their faces they read his text message. As a trio we decided to lay low until this monster was behind bars.

I replied to him as I walked down the hall back to my office.

Kendra: Is someone catching feelings? Your heart would shatter if something happened to me?

Detective Killian: I feel a connection between us. Plus, this is a living nightmare. I need you to be safe. Promise me?

Kendra: I promise. I am guessing you will be working a lot more.

Detective Killian: Sadly, my schedule will be filled until I can make sure the citizens of Las Vegas are safe from this monster.

Kendra: I understand.

I understood he had a mountain of work ahead of him. I was slightly bummed knowing it would be a while until we got time together again. But Detective Killian had to be the Las Vegas Superman.

Chapter 3

Homebound

This chapter contains:

Profanity
Substance use

Our typical end of the week relaxing is going to look a little different until they catch the suspect. Detective Killian can only advise was to lay low, but he cannot control what people do. We tossed around ideas for what to do to unwind. Finally, we decided on a chill movie, margaritas, and taco bar. Nick oversaw the movies, Tasha got to relive the past of being a bartender by creating drinks, and I got to cooking for the taco bar.

All of us were in our little world, Nick was helping me in the kitchen to set up the mini taco bar and Tasha was being Tasha- dancing and living back memories of when she was bartending back in the day. It was crazy to think that we were so happy in that moment. It felt like there was no danger in the world. When the streets of Las Vegas were dangerous, more dangerous than normal; a killer was on the loose. I wanted to reach out to Detective Killian and see if there was anything I could do but I also did not want to overstep and bombard him, making him think that I was needy. He had enough to focus on.

I had to shake the feeling of helplessness and focus on the present day. It was our night to relax, and I was quietly celebrating about the letter I received. I was not mentioning anything, but I wanted to get input on different options for what I can do with the inheritance. I had to come up with a way to gather input without blatantly putting it out there. I had to be creative and think of a way to ask this question.

After a bite of the first taco, I did a happy dance *"Damn this is good, if I ever magically get rich, I should open up a taco shop!"* in my head that as smooth of a way of bringing up large sums of money. Tasha laughed *"You could, I know what I would do."* Nick chimed in *"What is that?"* Tasha answered, *"Invest into bonds and ETFs."* I asked *"ETFs? What is that?"* Tasha replied *"Exchange-traded funds it is similar to mutual funds that you can invest in multiple stocks at once."* Nick interrupts *"Interesting, I know what I would do."* Tasha and I giggled and answered, *"What would that be Nick?"* He smiles *"Open my own strip club of course."* We all burst out laughing. We can see Nick opening his own strip club with the works.

Listening to the conversation I smoothly started, I was able to take mental notes of different options I could do. I wanted to educate myself more on what Tasha mentioned about the EFTs. I needed to be smart about my next move.

Nick knows how to pick out amazing movies, however I could not focus on anything. My mind was on the inheritance. I still cannot believe I was given that much. I think the next step to take would be to talk to a financial specialist to help educate me. I quietly pulled out my phone to check out my bank app to see if I could schedule an appointment online. I yelled *"SCORE!"* in my head it was done, appointment scheduled.

As I finished up on the application and closed out of it a smile danced across my face. A text message from Detective Killian.

Detective Killian: I hope you are staying safe, miss you.

Kendra: I am home, took your advice, miss you too.

Detective Killian: Good. Time to get back to work.

Kendra: Be safe.

The movie ended and we were just chilling, we had a good amount of energy, and the night was still young. We decided to end the night and get some needed relaxation time. Nick and Tasha took off and I locked up the house.

I didn't want to end the night so soon; however, a bath was calling my name. I drew up a bath with bubbles and a cup of Epsom salt. I even wanted to spoil myself by putting my towel and bath robe in the towel warmer. I turned on some relaxing music, tied my hair up in a bun, and slinked into the bathtub. The hot water relaxed the aching muscles and my thoughts cleared from my busy mind. I have a lot to think about over the next few days. However, this bath is helping me relax for the rest of the night.

After a half hour the bath water started to become chilly. I reached for the drain stopper to drain the bathtub and my warm bath towel wrapped around my body. I reached for the oil of course I did not warm up my oil, not everything can be perfect. I oiled up and did my facial routine, draping my warm bath robe over my naked body. The warmth relaxes my body enough to feel sleepy. I untied my hair and laid in my bed and cuddled up in my sherpa blankets. I turned on the television. Within minutes, I drifted off to sleep.

Sometime around two in the morning I woke up thirsty. Making my way downstairs for a drink, I noticed a shadow walking outside on the sidewalk. Sneakily, I made my way to the closest window to peak out of. I caught the backside of someone walking past. It was hard to see exactly what they looked like. But they seem to be in a hurry to get home. I cannot blame them, it is late. I made my way back upstairs to get more sleep.

By morning, I felt refreshed and ready to conquer the day. I had a checklist of everything I had to get done. When I stepped out something in my gut told me to scan the area. Which is weird because I didn't get any weird feelings from seeing that person walking in the dark night. I got in my car and sent a message to Detective Killian.

Kendra: Hey, do you have an idea of what the suspect looks like? I noticed someone walking in the neighborhood at 2 in the morning. I just want to be on the safe side.

Detective Killian: I will have an officer patrol your neighborhood. Just in case.

Kendra: No need, they did not seem suspicious.

Detective Killian: End of discussion, a patrol car will be there tonight.

A good morning ended up in me being annoyed with Detective Killian. I get that he wants me safe, but I think he is taking it a step too far. If I can handle being stalked, stabbed, and dragged through hell I can certainly handle my own neighborhood. I had to shake the frustration away. I decided to go to the gym and run some errands. While shopping, I decided to get some art supplies to paint. Since I am going to be homebound, I might as well keep myself entertained.

Later that evening, as demanded I noticed the officer patrolling the neighborhood. I scoffed as I looked out the window. I walked over to the kitchen island, poured myself a glass of wine, and opened the paint, paintbrushes, and canvas. I took a deep breath to clear my mind. It has been a few years since I picked up a paintbrush. Feeling the weight of the paint on the brush felt like an old memory.

I zoned out and kept placing different strokes on the canvas, mixing colors, adding different shapes. After a couple of hours of getting lost in the aroma of the paint. The canvas was painted with waves of colors and flowers floating down the river. I carefully moved the canvas to dry overnight. My arms reach over my head, and I stretch out. I guess it is time to head to bed.

I cleaned up my mess and checked outside before heading upstairs and like clockwork there was the patrol car making their way down the neighborhood. I rolled my eyes and made my way upstairs for the night.

Chapter 4

Yes Sir

This chapter contains

Profanity
Substance use
Soft BDSM

A couple weeks passed and although Detective Killian wanted us to stay home. I have an unhealthy diagnosis of cabin fever. I need to get out of my house this weekend or I will scream. Plus, Detective Killian has ghosted me. Honestly it feels as if he wanted to see how much of a puppet, I am by holding onto a leash and dragging me back.

Lunch time rolls around, I need to stretch my legs and get some food and caffeine in my system before I start to fall asleep. I poke my head out of my office and see Mindy walking back to her desk. With a mischievous grin I ask, *"I'm going to take a lunch break. Do you want anything from Café Rose?"* A smile crossed Mindy face as she sweetly asked, *"Can I have the new matcha cream drink they just came out with?"* I replied *"Of course! It is on me! Be back in jiffy!"* Tasha and Nick had lunch appointments with their clients, so I was going to be on my own.

I know better than to look down when walking but it is an ugly habit I cannot break. I opened the door not paying attention colliding with this tall blonde in a suit. I dropped my phone, and he dropped his coffee. Profusely apologizing to him, I ran inside and grabbed several napkins to clean up the mess we made. Frantically I said, *"Please let me repay you and buy you a new drink."* The quiet blonde replied with a soft chuckle, *"It is ok, I drink too much caffeine anyways."* I argued *"So do I, please it would make me feel better."* He smiled and nodded his head in agreement to having me buy him a replacement. We walked up to the counter, placing the order and walked over to the quiet blonde.

He smiled as I approached, handing my phone to me. I smiled as I took my phone back and introduced myself *"Thank you. My name is Kendra, you are?"* his smile was charming as he answered, *"Nice to meet you Kendra, my name is Asher."* We shook each other's hands and made small talk as we waited on the order. Although he was shy and quiet, there was something unique about him. I couldn't place my finger on it. His coffee came out before the rest of the order, and he had to get back into the office.

Fighting with myself in the head I spoke out *"Wait Asher! You seem like an interesting person here is my number if you want to catch up some time."* Smiling sweetly as I handed him my card. He takes it and puts it in his coat pocket *"I'll be in contact. Thank you for the replacement coffee, Kendra."* Watching him walk out of the café doors I could see a faint smile on his lips which made me smile. After a couple minutes my order was ready to go. I made my way back to the office wondering when I would hear from the mysterious Asher.

Walking up to Mindy her eyes lit up with joy seeing her drink being placed on her desk. Cheerfully she says, *"Thank you!"* The phone rang before I could answer so I mouthed you're welcome back to her. Lunch was refreshing and I feel as if I can finish the days task. Several hours had passed by as I got ahead on my tasks. Tasha and Nick swung by my door to see if I was ok. I was so focused I did not even notice I was well ahead of schedule and it being time for us to head out. Both Nick and Tasha gave me a concerned look. The kind of look that says we need to check on your mental health look. I smiled sweetly *"I am ok, I just got lasered focus today."* They looked at each other and then looked at me *"if you say so."*

Walking back to the parking lot we were catching up on the day's events that took place. I put my stuff in my car and stretched the day away I chimed into the conversation *"I have cabin fever from listening to Detective Killian, let's get out and have some fun."* Both Tasha and Nick answered excitedly *"GIRL, YES!"* We all smiled and laughed in random conversations as we tossed around ideas on what to do away from our houses.

Our top three choices to decide from was to go out to a new bar, movies, or the high roller with drinks and desserts at a nearby restaurant. Which two of the choices are right next to each other. We finally decided to go with the high roller and dessert option. All of us are excited about a somewhat calm night out with the gang.

Shockingly the drive home was peaceful. Most of the traffic was gone, my nerves were not on edge when getting home. Which was nice for a change. I placed my stuff down and checked the mail. I wandered over the fridge to figure out what to make for dinner. I couldn't make up my mind so girl dinner it was. I threw a bunch of different snack foods together on a plate. I sat down and decided to grab my phone to scroll on social media.

I had an unknown text message that was sent to me a couple hours ago.

Unknown: Hey! It's Asher

Kendra: Hey Asher! I am so sorry I was swamped at work and just got home. Not realizing my phone was silent.

I quickly saved his information. If I am honest with myself my heart was racing a bit to see what his response would be. I am still working through some stuff with Dimitri. My phone vibrated. I was surprised that he replied so quickly. I was a tad bit anxious to read his reply, in my head, I was preparing to be in trouble. Because that was what happened with Dimitri. But I was surprised when I saw his response. My heart was still racing, so before answering I decided to take a moment and do some breathing exercises.

Asher: I understand, I put my phone on silent as well. I am glad we bumped into each other today.

Kendra: I am glad we bumped into each other as well. Hopefully next time I will not need to buy you a new drink.

Asher: Maybe I can buy the next drink? I didn't mention this. But your eyes are breathtakingly beautiful.

I smiled at his message probably longer than what I should have. He sent another text message to make sure I was still there.

Asher: Did I scare you off?

Kendra: No, you didn't scare me off. I am not used to getting compliments about my eyes.

Asher: You don't get compliments? I would shower you in compliments daily.

My cheeks heated up and turned a soft red as I read his text message. I cleaned up my mess and headed upstairs to relax for the evening. Asher and I texted one another for several more hours that evening getting to know him. My face started to ache a little with all the smiling I was doing with each compliment he sent my way. Getting to know him was a highlight of my evening. When 10:00pm rolled around, Asher was determined to finish our conversation. Telling me I need to get my beauty sleep and it was bedtime. I am sure it was his bedtime, and he was tired. I was a bit tired as well. We said goodnight and shockingly I drifted off to sleep after turning my alarm on and placing my phone on the charger.

When morning came, I got ready and made my way downstairs. I had a bit of time to make my breakfast and coffee. I enjoyed the conversation I had with Asher and getting to know him. I tossed around for a minute before deciding to send him a text message.

Kendra: Good morning, Asher. I had a wonderful time getting to know you a bit last night. Hope you have a beautiful day.

Asher: Good morning, Kendra. I had a blast getting to know you as well. I know it is short notice. But may I ask you out to dinner?

Kendra: Dinner sounds perfect. When would you like to meet up?

Asher: Tonight, 6pm, at Old School 702?

Kendra: Sounds perfect, see you there.

Asher: I can't wait.

Butterflies flew around my stomach; I couldn't believe I had a date tonight with Asher. I was a bit excited to get to know him better. I made my way to the office to get my workday completed. My goal of going into the office nonchalantly failed miserably as my very poor poker face would not let me hide my smile. I was acting like a schoolgirl who had a massive crush and could not hide it.

Looking at my emails my office door opens with both Tasha and Nick standing there with their arms crossed leaning in the door frame ready to do some investigating on who the new man was that had me cheesing from ear to ear. I spilled the beans and told them what happened at Café Rose and the text messages between Asher and me. I even informed them that we had scheduled a dinner date for tonight. Nick chuckled *"Old School 702? Talk about being different and causal for a first date."* Tasha smacked him in the arm *"Shh, I think it is sweet and it takes a lot of stress off both of them when it is casual."* I scoffed in a playful tone *"remember my luck with men? I am happy with this being casual. Plus, he seems quiet, I am not complaining about that at all."* They could not argue that and shook their heads in agreement before dispersing back into their own offices.

The workday ended and it was time to get to my date. Before heading to the car, I sent a confirmation text message to Asher and started to touch up my makeup.

Kendra: Just wanted to double check. Are we still on for tonight?

Asher: Yes, Kendra. We are still on for tonight.

I smiled like a fool as I made my way to the restaurant. I parked my car and started walking up as I took the escalator up to the second floor; I saw Asher waiting for me with a single red rose.

His smile was warm and charming as he walked towards me *"Hello beautiful."* As he handed me the rose with his right hand. I accept the rose with my left-hand blushing softly *"Hello handsome, thank you for the beautiful rose."* I interlocked our arms together as we walked inside the restaurant.

We were seated towards the back near the kitchen. It was a busy night in the restaurant, so it wasn't the quietest place. Either the host could tell it was a first date or Asher gave the heads up before I got there when he checked in with them.

It was different with Asher, we connected on a different level. Communication was flowing between us as we got to know each other. There was no stress of being over the top and exciting. We talked about everything and anything under the sun. Asher also held on to his word and complemented me whenever he had the chance, but it was not the annoying type of compliments to get into my pants. They were genuine and from the heart. He would hold my hand which felt like a perfect fit in his. Brushing his thumb across my knuckles as he looked me in the eyes.

I forgot there were gentlemen out here in Vegas. It is a rarity if I come across them. But it was nice knowing not all men were horny walking red flags.

Asher played with my fingers as he looked down at the table after the waitress removed the final dishes *"I have had a wonderful night getting to know a wonderful woman."* I smiled softly as I laced our fingers together *"I will agree, I had a wonderful night as well getting to know such a handsome man."* He stood up and gave me his hand so we could leave. Asher reached for my hand as we headed towards the parking lot walking through the shopping center as slowly as possible. We acted like children, being a bit silly on the way.

Once we reached my car. Asher twirled me around into his arms with a grin on his face he leans in and whisper *"Text me so I know you made it home safe."* I giggled *"Yes sir."*

In a heartbeat his eyes darkened like I have never seen before in the short amount of time we have known each other. Asher growled with heavy beathing. I whisper *"Asher?"* He pinned me against my car, his body pressed against mine. As he stared holes into my eyes. I was tempted to kiss him, but I was also scared by how quickly he changed. Without even thinking, I grabbed his shirt as I stared back into his eyes. His shallow breathing, Asher had zoned out, he was fighting with himself in his mind. He took a deep breath and backed off from me.

Asher spoke in an ashamed tone *"I am sorry about that Kendra, that word gets to me."* I quickly grabbed his hand and laced our fingers *"You don't need to feel ashamed; I do not kink shame. If you wanted to kiss me, I would have accepted it."* Asher pulled me into a tight embrace *"I am respectful Kendra. I would love to kiss your luscious full lips. In time."*

I shook my head in agreement although I was bummed, I couldn't kiss him. We finally pulled ourselves from each other and I guess he could tell I was feeling a bit down about the situation. He leaned down and gave me a kiss on my forehead as he whispered, *"Be a good girl and text me when you get home safely."*

I smiled as I looked up at him. I am a sucker for forehead kisses. I got in my car and drove home. Once inside I cozied up on my chair. I sent him a playful text message.

Kendra: I am home sir.

Chapter 5

Contract

This chapter includes:

Profanity
Soft BDSM

A couple days have passed and no word from Asher. More than likely I pissed him off with the text message. It was fun while that lasted. It was an easy week at work with minimal things to do. Tasha casually strolls into my office and sprawls herself on to the couch. Laughing to myself, I finish my email to a client. *"Boring day for you as well?"* I ask. Tasha dramatically rolls her head and says, *"You have no idea!"* I chuckle *"We will have a night out soon."* Before Tasha could answer my phone dinged with a text message. Tasha perked up with curiosity *"And whom shall that be?"* she asked.

Asher: Sorry for being MIA. Can we meet for dinner?

I stared at the text message from Asher. Letting out a shallow sight *"It's Asher the guy who ghosted me."* Tasha sits up with a surprised tone *"What does he want?"* Putting my phone down on the desk *"He said he is sorry for being MIA and if we can meet for dinner."* Tasha took a deep breath *"Bitch it is free dinner, go."* I rolled my eyes and picked up the phone to respond to Asher.

Kendra: When and where?

Asher: Tonight, my place.

Kendra: Sure.

"It looks like he is cooking for me." I said to Tasha. Tasha shifted in her seat and before she could say what was really being said in her mind. My phone lit up with the address of Asher's home. I copied it and sent it to her. Tasha headed out

29

of my office as she got the text message of Asher's address *"Thank you!"* she yelled back.

The final hours of the day felt like they were dragging. With how slow it was at work, I honestly felt like getting into bed and sleeping the rest of the day away. But I know I had to meet up with Asher at his house. I had a little extra time to go home and change into more comfortable clothes. So, I quickly headed home. I threw on a pair of jeans, a nice blouse, and some comfortable slip-on loafers.

I decided to send him a quick text to let him know I was on my way. When I drove up to the high-rise condos on the strip, I was surprised that we did not run into each other more often. It was close to work and the places we go to practically daily. I checked in with the concierge and they instructed me to go to the twenty second floor. I thought to myself *"Great, I am going to be stuck in the elevator."* I have a slight fear of elevators. The jerking when going and stopping scares me.

The elevator finally reached the floor. My heart was pounding, and I felt lightheaded. I stepped out and took a moment before finding his door. Asher opened the door wearing dark denim jeans, black shoes, and a dark grey t-shirt. His blonde hair was slightly messy, and his smile was soft as he stepped aside to let me in.

"Come Kendra. Dinner will be done in ten minutes." Asher said as he placed his hand on my low back to guide me towards the kitchen. *"It smells delicious, I had no idea you could cook."* I said as I followed his lead. Asher smiled as he took a bottle of wine out of the refrigerator and grabbed a couple of glasses. *"I am a jack of all trades; I will probably surprise you in more ways than one."* Asher smiled as he poured our drinks.

My curiosity struck me, and I needed to know answers, so I asked *"Since you disappeared on me. What happened? Did I make you mad or uncomfortable with the text message of calling you sir."* Asher looked down at his glass for a moment before answering *"I am sorry for disappearing; I have been working on a project with my company for the last several months and we are in the final stages. I cannot go into detail about that because a lot is at stake. Kendra, you did not make me mad or uncomfortable. When you call me Sir it is very much of a turn on for me."* Asher waits for my response as I comprehend what he said. As the wheels turn and it finally clicking that he is into a BDSM lifestyle.

My eyes opened wide, and I looked at Asher with surprise. *"Oh! You are into...oh."* Asher chuckled as he saw that everything was starting to make sense. He responded *"I am respectful and live this lifestyle seriously. I also really like you, Kendra. Communication is important to me. I really want to kiss you and see you on a physical level, but I will not do anything until we have an agreement. It is obvious that you have no clue about this life."* I stepped back creating space between us to ask, *"What kind of agreement?"* Asher took notice of the space I put between us before speaking. *"It is a contract about our rules for this lifestyle."* My lawyer instincts kicked in *"I am single and not ready for a relationship, let alone something this serious. Especially since I am not educated or have ever lived in this world before."* Asher smiled and looked down. Before he could answer the timer went off.

Dinner was ready, a beautiful rack of lamb with mustard shallot sauce, roasted asparagus, and roasted potatoes. As dinner continued, I was still curious about this lifestyle of his. Mainly on the contract he wanted me to sign before anything further happens between us. Since the contract process can take a while for both parties to agree. I was half tempted to know about this lifestyle before being signed into a contract for God knows how long.

I thought to myself in a moment of silence and suggested to Asher *"I would like a crash course before getting into anything serious. I can type up an agreement on my terms for learning purposes only that you would follow. If anything was broken on said contract or I say I am done. I can simply walk*

31

away, and we never have to discuss this or talk to each other again." Asher sat back in his chair crossing his arms with surprise. *"I never had someone suggest that to me before. If you are interested, we can go to the office after dinner and type it up."* I smiled and nodded my head in agreement.

After finishing up a delicious dinner and cleaning up together. Asher took my hand and led the way to his office. He pulled up the word document so I can make the quick contract. I sat there thinking about what to write for a few minutes.

This contract is a binding document between two chosen parties on equal terms and understanding. Breaking this contract by either party will result in instant termination of the contract.

I, Kendra Beatmaker, will be learning the BDSM lifestyle as a submissive under Dominant Asher Campbell. This voluntary agreement will protect both parties involved. Anything pursued in the learning process that crosses boundaries that are spoken about will void said agreement.

Although boundaries will be on a learn as we go basis. The importance of using safe words will be used to determine new boundaries.

Safe Words are **Mango** for immediate stop and **Mentor** for yielding there is a question. This learning agreement will end without legal repercussions and both parties can go their separate ways at any time. If they feel they are incompatible as Dominate and Submissive.

We both quickly agreed on the understanding that this agreement contains. Asher made sure to print two copies for him and myself. He signed his name on both and I signed my name on both. I reached out to shake Asher's hand. He took my hand in his to shake and he pulled me into his embrace. Holding me tight as he stares at my lips. His eyes slowly rise to meet with mine then back down to my lips. Asher leaned down to kiss me. His lips were hungry, his tongue was

32

massaging mine teasingly as his fingers wrapped themselves tightly in my hair pulling me closer.

Asher's lips moved down my neck as he pressed himself against me. I let out a soft moan as he pushed me onto the desk, forcing my legs to spread with his knee. I started to take his shirt off and recompacted the biting back on his neck. A moan leaves his lips. Asher pushes me down on his desk reaching over my head and pulls a strap out tying my wrists above my head.

In a panic I started to try to escape but there was no way to get free. Asher glared over my trapped body in a low voice *"Calm down my little one. This is your first lesson."* I tried to calm down my breathing as Asher walked from one side of the desk to the other. He reached down into a drawer and pulled out some items. Looking around the room I take a deep breath before asking *"Is this my first lesson sir?"* Asher dropped his head back and ran his fingers through his blonde hair before letting out a growl. *"Yes, little one. I want to see you squirm."*

Asher unbuttoned my jeans and pulled them and my thong down just enough to expose my lips. Then he shoved my shirt up over my head so I could not see anything. I felt his fingers trace my bra finding the front clasp and exposing my breasts. *"Mmm, such beautiful breasts little one."* Asher said as he took a feathery wand from my sternum circling around each breast. The feathery wand tickled as it brushed over my nipple as it hardened. Slowly the wand danced across my exposed skin lower and lower it went. I felt it dance from my hip bone to the other. Asher gives a low growl before he takes the feather wand to the top of my barely exposed lips and tickles them in a pleasurable way. I let out a soft moan.

"Such a needy little one." Asher chuckles as he leaves me wanting for more. *"I want more Sir."* I quietly begged. *"Tsk tsk I did not ask you to talk."* Asher said as he reached into the cup of water and grabbed two ice cubes and began to massage my breasts and stomach running it over my needy

lips. I was panting, waiting for more. I tried to regain my thinking from feeling his ice-cold fingertips tracing along my body. I heard in the distance the flickering of a lighter. I could not see what was going on, but something told me it was ok to remain calm. Asher started to walk closer to me and dragged his fingertips around my body. Suddenly, I felt something hot on me.

The moment it touched my skin it became warm. I yelped and yelled *"What the fuck Asher!?"* He chuckled and calmly stated *"Relax little one, it is just a little wax."* My pulsating heart started to slow down. I tried to focus on what he was doing with each drop of wax. Asher's final drop of wax landed on my just above my vulva and my body jerked up as I yelled ***"Mango! STOP NOW!"*** Asher quickly removed the dropped wax that he dropped onto my skin, clasped my bra, and pulled down my shirt so I could see him.

I laid on the desk patiently waiting for him to release my hands. Asher decided to climb between my legs and hover over me. He looked down at my body and slowly back up to my eyes. Asher moved a strand of my hair behind my ears while licking his lips and staring at me. *"I am going to have so much fun teaching you little one."* Before I could respond Asher's lips came crashing down onto mine as he grinds his pelvis into mine forcing me to feel his hard outline. I let out the softest moan as our tongues intertwined with each other in harmony. Playfully biting each other's bottom lip. Asher grinds a little harder as he viciously attacks my neck and chest with kisses and bites here and there. I let out a yelp as he bit harder in some areas. His hands drag down my side as he lowers himself down to my clit. His fingers dancing across my pelvis moving slowly down to my lips to spread them apart to stare at my clit. His breath was hot hovering over my clit. Watching him intently as I wait for his next move. *"Lick me sir."* I begged.

Asher's eyes darted back up to mine as he growled. In a swift movement Asher flipped me onto my stomach and raised me up onto my knees with my pants pulled lower. He struck me with his hand forcefully. I yelped from the stinging sensation left by his hand. *"Naughty girls call me Sir. Are you a naughty little one?"* I was too stunned to speak as I tried to comprehend what was happening. ***"Answer me little one!"*** Asher demanded as he struck me even harder on the ass. I yelped even louder *"Yes sir"* I let out.

Asher growled, he reached down and grabbed something off the desk as I heard him drag it off the desk. Simultaneously a sound of a whip cracking and being struck even harder with multiple strands from a flogger. I was confused if I liked it or didn't. *"I..I...I..."* I was stuttering to find my words. *"Little one you have safe words we agreed on."* Asher said emphatically as he struck me again even harder. ***"MENTOR MANGO RELEASE ME NOW!"*** I demanded. Asher hurried as he released me my hands from the bondage that was attached to his desk.

I was fixing myself and I had so many questions rushing through my head at once. Stumbling to find my words *"I thought you were going to teach me not beat me!?"* Asher took a step towards me. I put my hand up and stepped back away from him, putting some distance between us. My thoughts started to drown me as I thought of Dimitri and what he did to me. I couldn't hide my fear. It was slapped across my face. Asher saw the fear in my eyes and sat down on his knees *"Kendra, I don't know your past, but something is troubling you. In the scene, I was not trying to hurt you. I figured sensational play would be a good start to break the ice in this lifestyle. I am sorry."*

Trying to comprehend what happened, I was unsure if I wanted to continue this agreement. Trying to grasp control of my breathing I was slowly slipping into a panic attack. Asher gets up and comes to me reaching out for my hands to guide me into a breathing exercise. I reached for his hands and followed his guide. Breathing in and out with Asher, I was able to calm down quickly. Asher pulls me into his embrace and envelopes his arms around my waist kissing me softly on the lips *"Get some rest Kendra. I want you to think about our*

35

arrangement. If you want to continue, we will. If not, I understand. I am here to take your lead."

Before I could say anything, Asher took my hand and guided me to the elevator and took me back down to the lobby. In a daze I walked out to my car. For several minutes, I sat there in silence reflecting on our agreement and the activities that took place.

Chapter 6
Dungeon

This chapter contains:
Bondage
Profanity
Sensation Play
Impact Play
Edge Play

The following day I was not in the mood to talk much. I was confused about everything. I felt like I was in a tug-o-war battle with wanting to learn about this lifestyle and staying with what I know is safe. The lifestyle was intriguing to me. The sensations I felt last night were confusing. I liked them and I did not like them. I am not sure if it was because it was not discussed or what. My fear of triggering a PTSD episode or a panic attack crosses my mind heavily. This is a lifestyle that is seen by many people as fun and enjoyable. I want to try it, but I don't want to be tortured as an excuse for pleasure.

Focusing on my work was not happening, I stared at my computer screen as a knock on the door snapped me out of my deep thought. *"What are you thinking about?"* Tasha says interrupting my thoughts. I sat there as I tried to think of a way to express what happened. I took a deep breath before answering *"Asher is into BDSM, I have never done it and we did some stuff last night that almost triggered me."* Tasha sat back and took a deep breath before answering. *"What you don't know about me, I am a Dominatrix with my partner. It is a lifestyle adjustment."* In total shock I stared at Tasha with my mouth dropped to the floor. Tasha reaches across the desk and closes my mouth *"This is a new lifestyle for you, do you have a contract? Did he perform aftercare? Do you have any questions?"* she said assertively. I blank stared for a couple of seconds before answering *"We made a learning agreement that will end whenever I want with safe words, I started to have a panic attack and he had me do some breathing techniques with me. I am confused on what to do."* I rubbed my face and eyes and held my face to make sure I was not in a dream. Tasha sat back and relaxed a bit saying, *"Oh thank heavens, he is not a total fraud."*

Confused by her statement I asked *"Fraud?"* Tasha answered *"Most people who try to get into the lifestyle don't take a lot into consideration and they can be frauds. Open communication and trust are key to make it work."* I sat there listening as she went into depth about the lifestyle she lives with her partner. I was horrified and intrigued by it all at the same time. We also talked for several minutes about last night and the emotions I felt.

My phone lit up with a text message from Asher. I was a bit hesitant to look at it. The banner notification showed part of the text.

Asher: Kendra, I need to know if you are ok.

I took a deep breath and looked up at Tasha. She smiled, gave me an assuring nod with her head, and said it was going to be ok.

Kendra: I am ok, I am just processing everything.

Asher: I am glad to hear from you. I know this can take time.

Kendra: I need a couple more days. Friday, can we meet?

Asher: Friday? There is a party we can go to!

Kendra: Sure.

I sat back in my desk and looked up at Tasha and said *"I told him I needed a couple more days to think this over. I told him Friday we can meet. And he suggested some party that was happening."* Tasha covered her mouth to hide her laughter *"I know of the party."* Confused I asked, *"You do?"* Tasha licked her thick lips and smiled softly at me before speaking *"Kendra, it is a dungeon party for those in the BDSM lifestyle. You will be exposed to a lot there; I think it would be good for you to see everything. I will be there and can be your undercover back-up. I will keep my distance, and you can give me a wink when we make eye contact to let me know you are ok."* I think about it for a few seconds before answering *"Deal."*

Throughout the week Tasha and I talked about every little question I had. I could not be more thankful for a friend like her as she has taken the time to educate me properly on what was about to go down on Friday. From videos to pictures, a ton of research. Tasha educated me enough to be able to walk into this party with confidence and not be fully culture shocked as soon as we entered. I also kept in contact with Asher and asked him questions periodically while we still got to know each other better. I was hesitant to build any emotion into liking him. He had a ton of great qualities, but a giant red flag was his lifestyle choice. I kept my walls highly built; he will have to be one of a kind to destroy them.

The night of the party we arrived at the Dungeon. Tasha kept her distance but coincidently crossed my path several times. I was highly impressed with her outfit of choice. She looked like Cat Woman in her leather bodysuit that zips. The breast area was cut low enough to barely show the areolas. She walked in confidently with her mask and thigh-high boots. She smiled at us as we walked in. I grabbed Asher's hand as he helped me out of the car. He pushed me against the car to kiss me softly and whisper *"I want your thong off before we enter."* I smile between kisses and whisper back *"They're crotchless."* I felt his knee buckle as he grabs my hips *"I can't wait to fuck you in that sexy little leather dress of yours."* I bite my bottom lip and grab his hands to take them off me to make him guide me into the party.

Walking into the party, I was nervous. This place was massive. We decided to check out the place before taking part in activities. We stopped at the bar and got a drink before we walked towards the first room. Looking around it looked like a strip club setting. There were a couple of stages with poles and booth seating surrounding them. A couple of pets took advantage of the stages and started to put on a show for their masters. So many people started to arrive, the outfits of choice varied as we went room to room. Walking into the next section of rooms there were blocked off rooms for couples only who do not share but watching was allowed. This area screamed safe to me. I whispered in Asher's ear "*I am ok with this room.*" Asher smiled "*Good little one.*" We continued further, heading upstairs where there was a watch room for gang bangs, there was a woman strapped to the bed. She was blindfolded, hands and feet tied to all four corners of the bed, and a gag ball in her mouth.

A man sat in a chair jerking himself off as several men used her for their disposal. On the speaker you can hear the man sitting down say "*You are such a good little cum rag.*" Asher pulled me down the hall, we passed a very open bathroom. Stopping in my tracks I hear Asher chuckle "*For those who like golden showers and potty play.*" I tried to bite my tongue to not say anything mean but my face turned into a disgusted look quickly. Asher laughed as he pulled me down the hall.

Before opening a very heavy door Asher looked into my eyes deeply "*Ready? We're here.*" I nodded as we entered a red lit room with black equipment surrounding every inch of the room. I scanned the Dungeon room; it was nothing like I have ever seen before. So many contraptions, cages, and devices. People dressed in full body suits with masks to nothing on. Looking all around in the dimly lit room I was intrigued by watching the others all around us. I stood next to a bird cage in the corner of the room, it was the contraption that was not being occupied.

Asher grabbed my hand and pulled me into his embrace to make me look at him. His pointer finger and thumb grabbed my chin and kept my face from moving. *"Little one it is not polite to stare."* He said in a low assertive voice. Before I could say anything, Asher interrupted me *"Little one, sit in the cage now."* My hands trembled as he held open the door to the bird cage. Asher's free hand was placed lightly on my low back as he gently pushes me into the cage and shuts it closed. I sat there looking around. From behind I hear a low growl near my ear *"You look so pretty in that cage little one."* My breath hitched in my throat as I looked around. A woman whose back was turned to us at the swing turned around. In embarrassment, I looked down and recognized the shoes. Slowly raising my eyes on the woman. It was Tasha, she was wearing a strap on over her cat woman suit fucking her partner who was in the swing. We exchanged winks, my nervousness was at ease knowing she was close by.

Several minutes passed by in the cage. Asher let me out and guided me towards a giant X contraption that was across the room that opened. Asher pushed me against it, locking each wrist and ankle. When Asher stood up his eyes showed flames of desire. His lips came crashing into mine. His hands roamed my body as I stood there helpless. Asher's hands caressed my ass and raised my dress up high as his kisses became aggressive. *"You look fucking beautiful standing there so helplessly little one."* Asher said as he pulled away and started attacking my neck with firm bites. I let out a quiet moan as he grabbed my breast pulling my dress down to expose me. My legs started to get wet from my pussy. I was enjoying Asher's hands and mouth ravaging me. My head fell backwards as he bit my nipples and sucked on them. I started to squirm. The wetness between my legs became greater. Asher's hand than came crashing down on my ass for moving too much.

Asher dropped to his knees as he stared at my wet lips. Licking his lips as he admires what was waiting for him. I tried to rock my hips towards him, but I was stuck. He leaned in closer; I could feel his breath right by my clit. I bit my lip waiting in anticipation. Asher's tongue plunges between my

41

lips and I let out a moan as my head rolled backwards. His tongue was magical, he rolled it in ways I have never felt before. My clit was swelling as he sucked on it harder. His tongue fucked my pussy faster and harder as my legs trembled. I was close to coming. Asher quickly pulled away and the urge to release was no longer there. *"You don't cum until I tell you to cum."* Asher demanded. I stood there as I tried to catch my breath. He released my ankles and wrists and dragged me to the next station.

Quickly Asher dragged me to the next station. It was an exam table with restraints screwed into the side. It looked like something I would see at my gynecologist office with more whistles on it. Asher lifted me up onto the table. He whispered in my ear *"If you cum, I will beat your ass at the next station."* I was stunned at his comment but shook my head in agreement. He strapped my hands and ankles down to the table. I took a deep breath and waited for the torture to start. Asher ran his hands over my body, he grabbed my tits, pinched my nipples, and then slapped them. I was turned on by the sensation. He then dragged one hand down my stomach.

My body ached for wanting to be fucked. He paused for a minute as he watched me close my eyes in anticipation. I let out the loudest scream the second he shoved his fingers into my aching pussy. He fucked my pussy with two fingers and then quickly added three and four fingers. My moans got louder as he started to pound my pussy with his fist. My eyes rolled back, and I couldn't control the screams of pleasure escaping my lips. *"DO NOT CUM LITTLE ONE!"* Asher demanded. He thrust harder and faster.

I could not help but release with the sensation of his fist and forearm fucking me. My walls pulsating around him as my core shook from exploding cum all over him. Asher shook his head in disappointment. *"Looks like my little one needs to learn a lesson."* He walks over and shows me the cum dripping from his arm. *"Let me lick it clean."* I said seductively.

42

I slowly cleaned my cum off his arm and sucked each finger clean. His eyes rolled to the back of his head as he bit his lip.

I was released from the exam table and taken to a couch that was on the other side of the room with many whips and floggers hanging behind them. Asher laced his fingers with mine. He spun me around and draped me across his lap as he sat down. I was facing down and clueless as to what whip he decided to grab for my punishment. I was a bad girl because I came all over his hand and arm. Chills ran down my body as his hand rubbed my ass. I took a deep breath before his hand smacked down my bare ass. I let out a loud *yelp*. *"Count loud and clear little one."* He demanded. *"**One**"* I answered loud and clear. Another impact of his hand even harder than before *"**Two**"* I cried out. I took a deep breath to hold in as I waited for the third impact from his hand.

I started to get lightheaded. Slowly I let the air out in my lungs and took another deep breath. Then I felt the most painful impact and loudest whip connecting with my bare ass. *"**Three**"* I said as tears streamed down my cheek bones. *"Good little one, you did a perfect job for taking this paddle."* Asher praised. His hand gently rubbed my ass cheek before letting me get up from his lap.

I took a minute before getting up from the couch. Asher stood up and took my hand in his with a proud tone he said *"Time for the finale little one. Are you ready?"* My body was aching in more ways than one. I asked *"Finale?"* Asher whisked me through the ocean of people to a medieval contraption. Asher showcased the machine and then handed me a blind fold. *"I know you need to cum again. You will cum on my cock this time. Little one you will be blindfolded so you cannot see a thing."* He slipped the blindfold on me and guided me towards the kneeling pillory. I felt like I was still in trouble and him fucking me like a medieval criminal. It was a bit uncomfortable. I could feel Asher's hands roam my body to let me know he was there. He hikes up my dress and spreads my legs with his legs.

I could hear his pants unzip; I could hear the opening of a condom wrapper. It was eerie how quiet it was, almost like I could hear a pen drop. Asher easily pushes his cock inside me. Thrusting nice and slow, feeling every inch of his thick massive cock. My eyes rolled back to the back of my head as he pulled himself out his tip resting at my entrance. He shoved himself in harder as he digs his nails into my hips rocking me back and forth in the pillory hitting the back of my head and chest. My moaning cries get louder and pleasurable. Feeling his balls slap my clit makes me instantly release all over him. Pulsating all over his throbbing, thick, massive, cock. His nails dig deeper into my skin. I milk his cock as hard as I can while matching his thrust. He lets out a moan as he bites down on my shoulder as his cum shoots into the condom. He slowly pulls out and kisses my body as he fixes my dress before releasing me.

Asher pulls me up into his embrace and kisses me passionately. *"You did wonderful little one."* I smiled and hugged him tightly. *"Thank you."* As I nuzzled into his neck. *"Time to go home and get rest"* he suggested as we walked out of the party. I scanned the room to see if I could see Tasha, but she vanished.

Asher was a gentleman but also a dirty freak. I was exhausted from tonight's adventure. On the ride home, Asher picked up a late-night snack and got a bottle of water for the two of us. It was like night and day with him. How he fucked me to how he treated me afterwards. I felt like a passenger princess on the way home. He walked me to the door and kissed me good night.

I changed into my pajamas and instantly crashed on my bed; I was so exhausted from everything that was done to me.

Chapter 7
Boundaries

This chapter contains:

Boundary Crossing
Impact play
Profanity
PTSD

Monday rolled around and I was surprised that I did not hear from Tasha or Asher. With what happened at the party it was certainly out of my comfort box. It was nice to reflect on everything. I strolled into work to find Mindy at her desk working away, Nick was in a phone meeting, and Tasha was in her office with a client. I started on my workday and before I knew it lunch rolls around. Nick and Tasha peeped their heads into my office so we could go to the café.

Once we got seated and ordered. Tasha bravely announced *"Kendra, how do you feel about the party?"* Nick's ears perked up *"Party?"* I choked a little on my water *"I, we, uh, the party was interesting."* Nick slowly turned to Tasha and said, *"She went to Dungeon?"* I interrupted *"How did you know?!"* Nick chuckles *"Kendra, I know **EVERYTHING** about you bitches."*

The entire lunch Tasha and I engulfed Nick and the world we experienced. From newbie to professional and everything in between we have seen and done. We finished up and started to head towards the door. As I opened the door to step out, I crashed into somebody as they were walking in. Wrapped in this strangers arms to prevent me from falling flat on my face. *"Oh God, I am so sorry!"* I looked up and noticed it was Asher. I smiled softly as he lifted me back to my feet. *"You should look where you are going Kendra, you could have gotten hurt."* Asher sounded annoyed with me. I looked down and excused myself and quickly left.

Tasha and Nick gave me a look and asked, *"Everything ok?"* simultaneously. Confused by Asher's words I tell them *"Yeah."* I got back to work but it was hard to focus. I was frustrated with Asher. Our agreement, the party, going MIA, and then acts cold towards me. Like what the actual fuck? I get that Vegas is hook up culture but what happened to actual fucking decency? I decided to let my emotions override and texted Asher.

Kendra: I am not sure what to think. But I did not appreciate the coldness coming from you at the café. I apologized it was an accident and you made me feel like shit. On top of that you disappeared since the party.

Asher: I was telling you what could have happened. If you took it wrongly that is on you. I was letting you recover.

Kendra: That! Exactly that. Your tone is cold. Did I fuck up? Can you inform me on what the fuck is going on?

Asher: Watch your cursing little one. I will see you on Wednesday.

Kendra: You are so fucking annoying. You cannot step away from the so called "lifestyle" to have a conversation with me.

Asher: Use your safe words.

Kendra: MENTOR MANGO

Asher: I will see you Wednesday.

I wanted to throw my phone at the wall. It is hard to make my blood boil and I was getting to that point. Asher and I had good chemistry. However, this man was driving me insane. There was no way that I could continue the agreement we had. The party was interesting and certainly something to cross off from the Kink Bucket List.

My frustration continued to grow throughout the rest of the day. At the end of the day, I decided to take matters into my own hands and drive to Asher's home. I know he said to come on Wednesday, but this contract needs to end tonight. I made my way to the lobby and because I had already been here before I was able to find out if he was home. I quickly made my way up to his door.

Asher's door was open, and he was leaning in the door frame. He was shirtless and in grey sweatpants. He looked annoyed as I approached. *"Little one, I said Wednesday."* Asher's voice was stern. I took a deep breath *"I think we should talk about this agreement."* Asher stepped out of the way and let me enter his home.

"What did you want to talk about?" he asked as we sat down on his couch. *"I don't think this lifestyle is for me."* I explained. *"Little one you are still in the learning stage."* Asher answered. *"Yes, I know. However, I feel like a sex object. Like nothing will go further with us than just this."* I spoke. He took a deep breath before leaning towards me. *"You are not a sex object little one. I want to be easy with you. I can be rougher if you like."* Asher said as he kissed me teasingly. I took a sharp breath in as Asher's words were tempting. Our lips locked and his hands entangle themselves in my hair. Pulling my head back he bites my neck here and there each bite getting harder until he reached my trap where he bit ever so hard making me moan.

Asher growls and starts to rip my clothes off leaving a trail towards the bedroom. Throwing me on to the bed he straddles me as his hands and lips roam my body aggressively. This was a sensation I had never felt before with him. The lower he goes the more his bites get more painful. Asher grabs a spread bar and locks my ankles in forcing my legs as far apart as they could go.

In a blink of an eye, he flipped me over a pillow to raise my hips. Asher ate my pussy from behind making me moan louder. Soaking my lips with his tongue as he buried his face to suck my clit like a starving man. Just as I was starting to cum, he rams his thick huge cock into my pussy and thrust as hard as he could. My eyes rolled to the back of my head as cum squirted out and drenched his cock with each pounding thrust. He flipped me onto my back as he held my legs in the air with the bar. *"Such a good little one, taking this cock like a whore."* Asher moaned.

His hands gripping my body pulling on my breast and slapping them. *"No!"* I yelled. His thrust became unpleasant as he did not like me saying no. *"Use your safe words."* His hand found my throat as he squeezed demanding me to use the correct words. I can feel the condom filling with his warm sticky cum. I tried to move my head from his grip. Asher smacked my tits again as he reached over to grab a knife between each thrust. He held the knife down to my sternum.

My vision began to blur, giving into my haunting past. I could feel sweat dripping down my temples and my breathing become uncontrollable. Everything was growing distant as I tried to pull myself out of the spiral back to the hell I went through with Dimitri. I felt trapped, was I going to get stabbed again? Was it my time to die? My mind was racing with thoughts a thousand miles a minute. Tears started to stream down my face as my heart felt like it was fracturing into a million pieces as it pounded against my chest.

The world turned grey as sharp sensations can be felt though out my body and the only sound, I could hear was the echoing screams in my ears. The flashback crested as I felt an intense stinging strike upon my face.

*"**MANGO, MANGO, MANGO!**"* I took the bar and kicked Asher's chest to get him away from me. I quickly unbuckled the straps. I grabbed a dress shirt that was on the chair near the door. Asher sat up and was trying to catch his breath *"**FUCK YOU! CONTRACT TERMINATED!**"* I screamed as I rushed out, grabbing my belongings and making my way to my car.

I passed by the concierge desk and yelled *"**Tell Asher I will mail his shirt to him, if he comes near me, he will see a restraining order!**"* Breathless in my car, I searched my purse for my prescription bottle. I quickly took my medication to help calm down my nerves before I took off driving. I texted the gang to let them know I was not ok.

Kendra: Met up with Asher, went to talk to end agreement. Ended up hooking up. He put a knife to my chest and struck me. Freaking out! Heading home.

Tasha: On my way!

Nick: See you at your house!

I tried to control my breathing, but I was worked up with fear. The thoughts that haunt me from when Dimitri tried to kill me are flooding my thoughts. I cannot think clearly, at the stop light, I frantically start patting my body to check for blood. Searching all over my chest and stomach. I can feel the warm liquid on my body. There was no blood, I took a deep breath when the car behind me honked its horn because the light was green. I panicked and screamed in response. Finally getting to my house. Tasha and Nick are at the garage waiting for me to pull in. I got out of the car, my face soaked in tears as they held on to me assuring me that I was safe and not in danger. Tasha started a shower for me, and Nick put my pajamas in the dryer so they could be warm when I got out.

After I washed away the disgusting feeling of Asher. Tasha and Nick wanted me to eat. I had no appetite *"Thank you, I will eat later."* I said as I excused myself to go lay down. Tasha and Nick looked at each other and then followed behind me. I laid down on my bed covering myself in my blanket up to my nose. Tasha and Nick joined me on each side sandwiching me in cuddles. I felt safe from the nightmare and quickly drifted off to sleep.

Chapter 8
Grocery Store

This chapter contains:

Finger play

After a couple of weeks have passed, I desperately needed to go grocery shopping. I started to make my way around the house and gather a list of everything that I needed to replenish. Honestly, I wanted to be lazy and look homeless, but something was telling me to put a little effort into my appearance. I decided to go wear black ribbed yoga leggings and a red ribbed crop top with a deep U to show plenty of cleavage. I wore my hair down and applied minimal makeup.

Usually, I like to get in and get out before all the chaos of people comes flooding in. Today, I decided to take my time and check out what was in the store because I needed to replenish a good amount of stuff. Walking up and down the aisle. I noticed I kept walking past this woman. She would take glances here and there. She was wearing a cute yoga outfit, so I decided to compliment her if she walked by me again.

When I reached for the laundry detergent another hand reached for the same one. I turned to see the woman reaching for the same laundry detergent. *"Oh, I am sorry, here*." I said with a soft smile. *"No, I am sorry!"* the mysterious woman said. I handed her the laundry detergent and took one for myself. *"I love your yoga outfit. Very cute"* I complimented her. She takes the detergent and softly blushes *"Thank you, my name is Lily. And your name?"* Lily says intrigued. *"I am Kendra, nice to meet you, Lily."* I reached out to shake her hand. She placed her hand in mine to shake but got distracted by my cleavage. Lily shook her head *"So, umm, I see that you wear yoga gear. I am an instructor at a heated studio. You should come check it out."* Lily says as she hands me her business card. *"That sounds like fun, I would like that if you were my instructor."* I said in a flirtatious tone. Lily looked down and smiled *"I can make that happen."* I handed her my card and told her *"Hopefully, I will see you soon."* We smiled at each other and started to go our separate ways.

After about an hour of strolling around, it was time to make my way home and put away everything. I connect my phone with my Bluetooth speaker. While I was dancing, putting items away, and washing the food I just bought my phone chimed with a text message with an unknown number.

Unknown: Hey it's Lily. I figured I would text you. So, you could have my number when you wanted to do a class with me. Nice meeting you today.

I smiled at the text message before replying. She seemed cute and I totally would not mind a good sweat session to detox my body.

Kendra: Hey Lily! I appreciate getting your number. When is your next class?

Lily: I am heading to the studio soon. What is your experience with hot yoga?

Kendra: umm Yoga wise decent and hot yoga total newbie. But I have been in a sauna.

Lily: If you have no plans, the studio is closed. I need to go and do some paperwork. But you can come test it out in private. So, you don't faint on me.

Kendra: I can do that. Text me the address.

Lily sent the address and I have seen this studio off Decatur and 215. It is massive. I could not believe that she owned this building. It had individual rooms, group rooms, showers, and so much. Lily was a successful yogi. The back door where she told me to meet her was locked. I let know I was here. Her smile was welcoming when she opened the door. *"I just got* the individual room turned on. It should only take a couple of minutes to be ready." Lily said. I returned the smile to her "That's perfectly fine Lily, we can get to know each other." I mentioned. Lily's cheek turned a soft pink as she looked away. I smiled softly and thought it was sweet.

Lily took me on a tour of her massive building. I was amazed by her success. Each room and hall Lily was beaming with pride. Our chemistry flowed easily as we giggled and talked like school age girls. The friendship we have created felt like it has been there for years.

We finally made it up to the individual room she had prepared for us. "It is at a lower temp than we normally work with, I would hate to have you faint on me. Lily mentioned but mumbled something under her breath "I would like to be your hero." I tried to pretend I didn't hear the second part, but I responded to the flirty remark "As long as you catch me." I took a leap of faith and went bold.

Lily sat on the floor across from me on the mat and I sat in front of her. She showed me how to properly breathe as my body adjusted to the heat. We went through basic stretches so I could get acquainted with the setting. I forgot to eat, and I started to feel funny. I reached for Lily's hands, and she laced our fingers together. "Are you ok?" she asked, leaning in close to my face. "Yes, just takes a bit of getting used to." I answered as I leaned a little closer. Lily leaned in and gave an innocent kiss on my lips. Taken back from her bold move I sat back. Lily quickly apologized "I am sorry, you are breathtakingly beautiful, and I must have read the signals wrong." I leaned in and placed my hands on her legs to brace myself before answering. "No, you are perfectly fine, I just never kissed a woman before." We both smiled. Our cheeks flushed in red tones, you could not tell if it was embarrassment or from the heat of the sauna.

I rolled my head in a slow circle before leaning in and pulling Lily into a sensual electrifying kiss. My hands placed on the side of her face as the intensity of our kiss grows. Her hands draped over my hips as she pulled me in closer teasing my tongue with hers. Our hands slowly trace each other's curves. Her hands grab the back of my neck to hold me closer nibbling on my bottom lip. I pulled her on top of me between my legs and started to kiss Lily intensely. Our hands roamed and grabbed each other's ass and breasts. Squeezing firmly, we both let out a soft moan. I wanted to pull her clothes off and have my way with her. But I started to feel faint. Lily adjusted herself and said *"We need to get out of here and get some water now. It has been far too long to be in here."* I smiled and agreed, nodding my head.

We sat down together and drank some water to cool down on a wall booth. Our friendship has taken off in more ways than one. When I started to feel better, I looked up at Lily who was already standing. I had no idea how she could be nonchalant about sweating in a sauna. Just before I stood up Lily straddled my lap and attacked my lips with hers. I could not control the moan that escaped my lips as her lips and tongue danced with mine.

Between kisses Lily whispered, *"I like hearing you moan."* What she didn't know is that I wanted to hear her moan as well. I had one arm around her waist and the other hand roamed and squeezed her breast hard. Lily let out a yelp before I traced my hand down over her pants as I started to gently rub her pussy. A soft moan escaped her lips. My world exploded as I heard the sweet sound escape her beautiful full lips. I started to massage a little harder. *"Touch me more"* Lily moaned. I slipped my hand into her pants as my fingers danced between her wet lips. I played with her clit as her head rolled back moaning louder with each finger, I slipped into her. I was so turned on my legs started to become soaked.

After several minutes of Lily being pleased and letting out lovely melodies she finally came on my fingers. I pulled them out and started to suck it clean. *"You taste so sweet."* I seductively said.

Lily kisses me one last time to taste herself on my tongue. I could have thrown her on the booth and figured out how to fuck her. The nearby door opened, and her cleaning crew arrived. She jumped from me and greeted them. She gave me an apologizing look and I mouthed. *"It's ok, I promise."* Lily mouthed back *"Thank you."*

I gathered my belongings so Lily could get back to work. Never in a million years did I think I would ever get with a woman. Honestly it was the best feeling in the world. Lily was different, we connected on so many levels in such a short time. It felt like we were long lost friends the way we connect. Our conversations flowed effortlessly, as if we had known each other for years. There was undeniable electricity between us. Like there was a magnetic pull between us, an unseen force as tangible as the air yet as undeniable as gravity itself. When Lily's eyes locked with mine, we had unspoken communication. I was not complaining about the invisible thread pulling us closer inch by inevitable inch.

The entire drive home I felt like I was floating on air. All I could think about was Lily. I could not wait to see Lily again. I started to become addicted to her. I needed more time with her, to taste her lips again, to feel her touch one more time. Lily felt like home.

Chapter 9
Heated

This chapter contains:

Temperature play
Finger play

Over the next couple of weeks our friendship could be described as twin flames and unbreakable. There was little to no stress, labels, drama, or each of us trying to impress each other. It was refreshing. We have only had a handful of make out sessions. Because she knows I am new to this. I want to take it slow with my previous history. Granted all the drama and most of my trauma has been with men. I am tempted to try to take it further tonight.

We are meeting at her studio for a private one on one session. If I am being honest, I cannot get my mind out of the gutter. I have gotten so used to my world being rocked right away that I want her to bend me in every position and have her way with me.

Arriving at the studio, I decided to be more seductive with her when I saw her. Lily leaned in for a hug while she let me in. I gave her a hug but as soon as the door closed. I pinned her against the wall and passionately kissed her as I pressed my pelvis against hers grinding slowly as our kiss deepened. A soft moan escaped her lips as she pulled me closer to her. I pulled away and smiled devilishly. *"Well hello to you too Kendra."* She said as she adjusted herself. *"Hello Lily. Before the session can you let me go in and set up? I have a surprise for you."* I mentioned. Curiosity rose from Lily as she looked at me with one eyebrow raised. She cautiously agreed, *"Ok, sure."*

I go into our sauna room and set it up. Little did she know as she was waiting outside the door. I was stripping down and taking off every piece of clothing. Trying to figure out what pose to greet her in. She knocked to see if I was ready. I hurried and got into Siddhas Ana. *"Come in"* I say. She cracked open the door and her eyes scanned my naked body. *"Oh, fuck Kendra. I cannot believe my eyes."* Lily says. Lily walked in and stood at the top of my mat staring at me. I decided to put on a show. I spread my legs to show her my already wet aching pussy. I slowly moved into Ananda Balasana to let her get a better view of what was waiting for her. Lily dropped to her knees and wrapped her arms around my hips and started to devour my pussy. Her tongue danced around my clit in circles making me scream in pleasure. Each finger Lily inserted into me I moaned louder. My clit swells as her lips nibble and suck on it. I started to explode in her mouth. Lily hums making it a vibration on my clit driving me over the edge of squirting. My legs drop as she finishes her meal. I started to rip off her shirt and pants.

Down on my knees I praise her body; Lily moves her body into Chakrasana exposing her pussy at the perfect height of my mouth. I kiss her right thigh and up her left thigh. I lick her lips gently. As I got more comfortable with eating her pussy. I started to go deeper. Tongue fucking her harder. My hands glide up her body as I squeeze her tits. I got comfortable making out with her pussy. Sucking her clit and massaging it with my tongue. She came in my mouth; her juices were sweet. I tried to control myself from turning into a savage animal.

Lily laid down on the mat and I climbed on top of her. Kissing up her body nibbling here and there as I climbed up her body hearing her moans. I muffled her mouth with mine as I kissed her like a savage. Massaging our tongues aggressively as I grab her breast and squeezed them in my hand. Attacking her neck with my lips as her fingers rub my clit. Us moaning in harmony. She rolls me over and gets between my legs. She lifted one of my legs in the air and straddled my pussy. Rocking back and forth her lips on to mine. My eyes roll to the back of my head in pleasure as I feel the euphoric sensation of riding my pussy.

56

Our bodies convulse as we come into synchrony. Our bodies intertwined like dancing cobras on a slip and slide. As our cum mixes our bodies start to shake from weakness. We both giggled and kissed one last time. *"Let's go recover."* Lily suggested. She grabbed my hand and led the way as we stopped and locked lips every few steps. I decided to take the lead and drag her into the shower stall and turn on the water. Our lips are locked as the water drenches our bodies. Our fingers tracing each other's bodies and fingering one another gently. Lilly pinned me against the wall as we lifted one leg onto each other and we grinded against one another moaning in each other's ear as the shower drowned out the noises of our lips wrestling each other as we came.

The water turned cold while we kissed and cuddled in the shower. That was the most we have ever released before. The sensation of exhaustion and being energized was hitting us both hard. I didn't want to leave her, but Nick sent a message.

Nick: Tasha is busy, I hate asking. I am stranded and need help. Can you pick me up? My car broke down.

I let out a semi-disappointed sigh and got dressed. *"I am sorry, Nick needs my help. He is stranded."* I mentioned. *"Go be an amazing friend babe."* Lily said.

Kendra: No problem. On my way. Send your location.

I put in the address and went to go save Nick. I arrived when the tow truck got there. Nicked looked me up and down and gave me the look of you naughty whore you just got your brains fucked. I rolled my eyes at him as he tried to confirm if I got laid or not.

Once we got into my car. Nick screeched *"**BITCH WHO DID YOU FUCK BECAUSE YOU ARE GLOWING!**"* I laughed and tried to divert the conversation. But it was no use. Nick kept asking nonstop. *"Okay! Lily and I had the best mind-blowing sex ever."* I said with a smile and my cheeks blushing red. I have never heard Nick squeal like a little schoolgirl. He was asking so many questions on the drive back to his place. I could not keep up with them. I tried driving as fast as I could to get him home sooner so the questions would stop. It doesn't help that I was also starving from the intense work out I just had.

Finally, I was able to kick Nick out of the car so all the questions could stop. I started to get hangry and annoyed. When he got out of the car he yelled *"THANK YOU BESTIE! WELCOME TO THE DARK SIDE!"* I laughed as I pulled out of the driveway.

I was starving after the sexy sweat session I had with Lily. I was craving a juicy cheeseburger with the works, onion rings, and a cookie dough milk shake. I quickly made my way to Smash after placing an order on their app. I did not even leave the parking lot before I dug right into eating. I sat happily in my car as I ate my post sweat sex meal in peace and quiet. I pulled my phone out to send Lily a quick text message.

Kendra: Today was perfect, just like you.

Lilly: I cannot wait to see you again.

I smiled as I looked at her reply. I could not believe how lucky I am that our paths crossed. My mind danced with the ideas of how our future could go. I guess after being stabbed by an evil monster the universe was making a path for me to find my special someone. I had no idea it was going to be a queen. I was not going to complain about it. Lily had me in complete awe, as I marveled at the serendipity that led our lives to intersect. With the short amount of time, we have spent together I have felt deep appreciation towards her and everything we have shared up to this point. It was truly humbling and exhilarating.

While reflecting on the serendipity of us meeting and recognizing the pure luck in finding someone who not only understood me, but her soul also shared similar dreams and future goals. I felt a sense of responsibility to take it to the next level. I finished my meal and cleaned up my mess. I had to think of a game plan to move it to the next level.

Chapter 10
Missing

This chapter contains:

Anxiety
Death

Days have passed and I have not heard from Lily. I was wondering if I was the problem. Did I do something to make her angry? Maybe she is busy, I know she mentioned something about events that were coming up and having to do recertification training for several of her employees. I tried not to think about it too much. I tossed around ideas on how I could make her feel less stressed and how I could possibly take our relationship to the next level. But I froze, I could not think of a way to make her feel special, she was easy going and I didn't want to ruin my chances of making her feel extraordinary. I had to think of something out of the box.

When I got to the office, Mindy informed me of a couple of voicemails from my clients. Making Lily feel extraordinary had to be put on the back burning for the moment. I had a couple of court cases coming up this week. So, I had lots to do in preparation that needed my attention. Time slipped away while I was busy working so that I did not even bother to check my phone. When it was time to go, I decided to sit back and pull my phone out to check on Lily. Nothing. Disappointment started to fill my head. Ugly thoughts started to fill my head. I know I probably had fallen too quickly for her, or I am completely desperate to find love. Failing this potential relationship could not happen. If it did, I could tell it would destroy me harder than finding out my ex cheated on me.

Tasha walked by and noticed I was not sitting quietly in my head. *"Are you doing ok Kendra?"* Tasha said with curiosity as she sat down on the couch in my office. I sat there staring at my phone for a couple of minutes before answering her. *"Not really. Lily has not answered me. I don't know if I pushed it too far with her."* a disappointed tone escaped my lips. *"Well, you did mention how she was busy with events and recertification training. She might be the type to isolate herself until things are checked from her to do list."* I let Tasha's words sink in and bring me back to reality. *"I guess you are right. I need to stay focused for these cases."* I shook off the feeling of abandonment and gathered my things to walk out to the car with Tasha. We started to talk about what to do this weekend and tried to come up with a couple of ideas before presenting them to Nick. We jotted down a couple of places before taking off. I didn't want to go home but I also didn't want to seem like someone who was obsessive and stalkerish.

I decided to kill a couple of hours at the bookstore and get a couple of new steamy dark romance novels, a new cookbook, and a relaxing eye mask that you can have cold or warm. It was nice walking around and seeing everything that they offered. My stomach started to growl; it was time to go home to make some dinner.

Thankfully the new cookbook had a recipe where I had everything already at home. This rarely happens, so I took it as a sign that it was going to be a good night. I flipped the page to Tenderloin Steak Diane, poured a glass of red wine, turned on some relaxing music, and started to make this delicious meal. My kitchen was filled with delicious aroma. The first bite was so mouthwatering my soul did a happy dance while I ate.

After cleaning up I decided to head to bed and start reading one of the new books. Around 3 chapters in my eyes lids started to feel heavy. I put my bookmark in and turned off the lights.

The following days come and go and still no contact from Lily. I gave up trying to hear from her, it was time for one of my trials. I decided to shut off my emotions with her and focus on my work. Thankfully, the trials I had this week were simple divorce cases with no children. When I put my focus into my work my clients always succeed. So, it felt great that they accomplished their goal and have a newfound freedom. It made me feel good and helped me forget about my personal life for a while.

By the time Friday came around the gang and I decided on checking out a new tapas place. We heard great reviews of their food and cocktails. All of us were on board needing this time to relax. As we met up in the parking lot, my phone started to ring. I was in shock to see Detective Killian calling me. I answered, "*Hi stranger, how can I help you.*" He took a deep breath before answering me in a direct tone. "*Kendra, can you come by the station tomorrow?*" I was confused by his request. "*Of course, is everything alright?*" I answered cautiously. Detective Killian paused "*Yes and no, I have a couple questions to ask you when you get here. Nine sound, ok?*" I was thrown off by his answer "*Yes, I will be there at nine.*"

Nick and Tasha looked at me with confusion as I hung up the phone. "*Detective Killian wants me to come by the station at nine tomorrow.*" I said with a stunned tone. "*Why?!*" They said in unison. I shrugged at their question. In my head I was having a panic attack from his hot and cold answer. Was I in trouble for something? Was one of my clients in trouble? Did one of my clients get arrested? A hundred questions rushed through my head as we sat down at the table. I tried my hardest to engage and be present with my friends, but my mind could not focus because I was worried about what Detective Killian wanted.

I guess Nick and Tasha caught on to the fact that I was focused on what was going to possibly happen tomorrow and not on the moment because they were able to tell our waiter to make my drink extra strong. I took one good swig and my eyes opened. When I tasted the heavy pour of vodka Tasha chuckled and Nick decided to look in a different direction. I took the subtle hint to put tomorrow's worry onto the back burner of my brain. I became more engaged into our evening dinner just in time when the food arrived.

Our mouths started watering as our waiter brought the stuffed dates, baked goat cheese, firefly fries, patatas bravas, meatballs, and poori and chicken curry bites. Everything was delicious with the flavors bursting in our mouths. We became so stuffed and happy from everything. Even though dessert looked delicious we all had to decline the offer. Before leaving we left a 5-star review on their social media accounts and made sure to take extra care of our waiter when the bill was paid. We slowly made our way out to the parking lot and said good night to each other as we headed home. It was a calm night off the strip. I knew of several events going on, so it was nice to have open roads on the way home.

Morning came and I was fighting a panic attack before heading to the station for questioning. I decided on a more casual business look to go into the station this morning. Black capri slacks, a light pink blouse, and slip on loafers. My heart was racing so much, I decided to skip out on coffee. I did not need a heart attack today. I grabbed everything and headed out the door.

When I arrived at the station, I checked in with the front staff and they contacted Detective Killian to come get me to go to his office. *"Kendra, this way please."* Detective Killian said in a cold business-like tone. I followed him straight to his office. The door shut as I sat across from his desk. *"What is going on Detective Killian?"* I asked cautiously.

Detective Killian took a deep breath *"Do you know this person?"* He pulled up a picture of a crime scene photo. I was frightened to my soul when I saw who it was *"Oh my god, that's Lily!"* I screamed. *"Her parents placed a missing person's report, and she was found a couple days ago in the dumpster outside her studio. When we searched her place of business, your DNA was found."* Detective Killian said with a blank stare. I started to cry I cleared my throat before answering him *"We are friends, were friends. She told me that*

she had several events happening and that she was going to
be busy. I had a trial and figured she needed some time.
Never crossed my mind that this would happen!" I pleaded.
Detective Killian grabbed the photo and said *"I know you are*
not at fault, if you remember the serial killer we are looking
for, he left his signature trademark on her. I need you to be
extra cautious when you are out and about." I shook my head
in agreement as tears drenched my cheek bones.

Such a lovely person is now gone forever. My heart shattered
into a million pieces. After receiving the news. Detective
Killian held my hand in silence. *"Is there a way you can give*
her parents my information so they can contact me? I would
like to know about her funeral information and help any way I
possibly can." I tearfully cried. *"I will make sure they will get*
that information; I am truly sorry about this." His voice was
filled with a promising tone.

I walked back to my car almost soulless. The pain of losing a
special friend tragically is like a shattered mirror, reflecting on
memories that once held endless joy. Each shard of glass
represented all the moments of laughter and experiences we
had together tinged with the ache of absence now that Lily's
life was taken viciously. This monster needed to pay for what
they had done to all the innocent lives they had taken.

I sat numb in my car reflecting about everything. The precious
moments and now the tragic news. My phone chimed it was
the group text.

Tasha: Any updates?

Nick: Do I need to get your lawyer?

Kendra: Lily is dead.

Chapter 11
The Funeral

This chapter contains:

Funeral

The next day I sat there in my bed experiencing a profound numbness and a sense of being lost, the weight of grief after a significant tragic loss is weighing heavily on me. Every emotion seems muted and navigating through daily life seems like a chore drifting through fog without any clear directions. Although our friendship was fresh, Lily and I bonded quickly. I attempted to move forward with my day, but every step felt as if it was treading through heavy mist. The uncertainty of each step and knowing their absence made my heart ache more. I knew this delicate journey was going to be a slow process to overcome. Lily would want me to move on.

Several hours passed and my phone rang with an unknown number from out of town. *"Hello?"* I answered *"Hi is this, Kendra? My name is Olivia, Detective Killian said you are, I mean were friends with my daughter, Lily."* A heartbreaking crack was in Olivia's voice as she spoke. *"Yes, Olivia, I am Kendra. I am terribly sorry for meeting like this. Is there anything I can do?"* I said as I choked on the words. *"Lily was a simple girl, she wanted to be buried as a tree to give back to nature. We will be holding a small service next Saturday right inside the Mountains region."* Olivia's voice trembled. *"Ma'am I will be there."* I said as a single tear rolled down my cheek. We spoke for a couple more minutes. It is painful losing a friend, but I could never imagine being in Olivia's shoes; being a mother who must bury their child before them makes my heart shatter even more.

I started to look up local florists and try to find the hippiest, most beautiful, environmentally friendly flower arrangements. Thankfully, I was able to find a florist to work with me. I placed the order with them and started to feel a bit of ease. For my mental health, I decided to relax as much as I possibly could. Work will be crazy next week and then the funeral. I need to be on my game as much as possible.

Days have come and gone amid a hectic work week preceding Lily's funeral; tasks pile up like an overwhelming stack of papers. Trying to balance my professional responsibilities while grappling with the loss of Lily has been demanding like a delicate dance. From back-to-back meetings, deadlines, and being an emotional wreck has weighed heavily as I prepare for this farewell ceremony.

When Friday evening arrived, I dreaded the next morning. I knew I was going to have to say good-bye forever. I decided to pour a huge glass of wine and snuggle on the couch with a blanket and pillow. I cried so much that I have no more tears left. I had to swallow the pill of acceptance and face reality. I decided to grab my notebook and pen to start writing a letter to Lily.

Lily,

I'm sitting here writing this letter. The ache in my heart mirrors the void your absence has left behind. Knowing your tragic departure has cast a shadow on the landscape of our beautiful memories, and the echoes of laughter we once created together now linger in the silence. It is surreal to write down a farewell, knowing that the ink on this paper cannot bridge the gap between here and wherever you are. Your spirit, however, remains intertwined with the essence of our friendship and romance, a timeless connection that even the finality of goodbyes can't serve. In this tapestry of life, you were a vibrant thread, weaving joy, and warmth into the fabric of my existence.

Your kindness, humor, and unwavering support painted the canvas of our friendship with hues that even with time will never fade. I find solace in the countless moments we shared.

Your laughter echoes in the air, the silent understanding between us, and the unspoken bond that transcended words. I miss you with every fiber in my heart. And though your physical presence is no longer here. The imprint you left on my heart is indelible. I will forever carry the memories and lessons we shared in this short time. And use them as a guiding light through the journey ahead. Lily, may you find peace in the vast expanse of eternity, and may the memories we have shared be a source of comfort.

Love always,

Kendra

I slept terribly that night but when the sun peaked through my curtain. I knew it was time to make the journey to say goodbye. Slowly gathering my belongings and letter to Lily, I stared at my door before embarking on an ominous stroll to my car to go to Lily's final resting place. The drive was quiet, for the first time in a while my brain was kind enough to give me a break from thoughts that have been drowning me.

Driving up the mountain, I was confused as to why she wanted to have her final resting point in the desert. One thing I learned was to trust Lily's process. Up the driving trail roughly thirty minutes into the mountains I reached the destination. I stepped out of the car and gazed upon the scenery. It was beautiful and peaceful. Butterflies danced in the sky and birds chirped a lovely melody. Even though it was midmorning the sun kissed the ground sending warm hugs that envelope you. The serene landscape brought a sense of peace. Looking around as Lily's loved ones gathered around her honorary tree.

Lily was a simple soul who wanted nothing but peace and happiness. Though I only knew her for a short time, I listened to all her friends and family express their memories both happiness and sorrow. It felt like I have known her a lifetime. Everyone was able to grab a couple of flowers off the flower arrangements. At the end we danced around her tree sprinkling them around her as a wreath.

After several hours of spending time in her final resting point. People slowly started to leave. Lily's sister had to guide her parents away from Lily's tree. It was a heartbreaking view to watch to see a beautiful family leave almost soulless. I decided to sit beside her tree and read her the letter. I needed a couple of minutes with her to read the letter I wrote. I figured I would be a blubbering mess with tears. Shockingly, I was able to read it out loud with a sense of peace. I know I am saying goodbye. But I will be back to visit her. I decided to dig a little hole next to her tree and bury the letter with her. I blew her a kiss and wiped as much dirt off my hands as possible and started my journey home.

Come bedtime, I tossed and turned. I felt peace at the funeral. But my dreams say otherwise. I was transported back in time, back to Lily. I heard her laugh and felt her touch. Back into her arms. *"I'm at peace."* Lily whispered as she softly kissed my lips. I started to cry hysterically *"I couldn't protect you, who did this to you?"* I cried. Lilly wrapped her arms around me to console me. I wanted that coward behind bars, I wanted Lily back! I buried my head into her chest holding her tight, desperately wanting to hear her heartbeat one more time.

Darkness surrounded me. I could no longer feel Lily and felt her voice drifting further and further away. I curled myself into a fetal position and quietly cried the rest of the night away. Thinking to myself, the world feels like a vast, echoing space, and I am standing in its center. I am alone, utterly alone. Being left behind and abandoned on a path that I clearly thought I was supposed to be on. Only to be veered away to leave me stranded in silence.

I stood there in darkness, the quiet is deafening, wrapping me like a shroud. I try to reach out hoping and praying Lily would come back and give me a hand to grasp. Nothing, only the cold touch of my own solitude. I should be used to this sensation as it was something I have felt with my ex. This void seems different.

Nights are the hardest as it is a reminder of isolation that consumes me. I lie awake in bed as my thoughts spiral, wondering how it came to this, such tragedy. When I went to sleep, I called out for Lily to come to my dreams. But I was left with emptiness.

I know I had to come to the realization that her spirit probably found peace. I needed to stop being selfish no matter how hard it was. I needed to let go and let her be free. She had suffered enough with her tragic death. She didn't deserve any of it. I just wanted to know when the pain stopped.

Chapter 12
Birthday

The chapter contains:

Profanity
Substance use
Threesome

Weeks passed; I was able to move smoothly through the grieving process. There were a couple of times that I lost all control, but it happens.

March is a special month; it is my birthday month. I know many people have the usual festive spirit when it comes to celebrating their birthday. I on the other hand have a subdued demeanor. I guess you could say it is pointless, but I lost someone very special on my birthday a few years back. My beloved fur baby who I had grown up with. A time I used to look forward to just reminds me of when they were run over and left for dead. At the office, I noticed a bouquet of flowers and chocolate from my favorite candy store. The card read.

We want to see you and celebrate you, Darling!
- Ace and Andy

My eyes lit up with joy and my heart smiled for the first time in a while. I honestly thought I would never hear from them since they went on tour. I sent them a quick text message.

Kendra: You guys! The flowers and chocolates made me so happy! Thank you so much!

Ace: You're welcome beautiful!

Andy: We are coming into town soon for a concert and we need to get together! Dinner?

Kendra: That sounds amazing! I cannot wait!

Maybe this birthday will be different. If I stay busy, I might be able to make it through my birthday without crying my eyes out. I decided to be naughty and savor a couple of candies. A brief retreat into sweetness. Each piece dissolved onto my tongue, releasing bursts of flavors that transported me momentarily into a realm of simple life and delightful indulgence. I sent them another text message before turning my focus on the meeting ahead.

Kendra: My delicious treat transported me to a happy place. Thank you so much.

Ace: No problem sugar!

Andy: Many more are heading your way!

Kendra: Guys! You know how to make a woman feel special.

Ace: Xoxo

Andy: Only for you!

It has been a while since I have heard from the dynamic duo. With everything going on in my life, it certainly cheered me up. Part of me doesn't want the attention and then part of me feels like I deserve it. They have always been amazing. Plus, if I am being honest, I miss them. While answering emails my mind kind of wandered away. I wonder if we can do another session of just the three of us.

My workday was dominated by the typical meetings, emails, and phone calls. Even though I tried my hardest to stay on the task. I couldn't have the comment from Ace and Andy linger in the back of my head. It was certainly the perfect distraction

I needed. The anticipation of what is to be unfolded certainly raised my body temperature a bit.

Nick and Tasha decided to swing by the office for a quick break and go over some plans they had come up with for my birthday. It is a good thing that I don't plan what I want to do because with their plans I would not have time to even catch a break. I know by the end of the month I will be exhausted. But something inside of me told me not to care.

After several hours at work, it was time to head home. I had a feeling that something or someone was waiting for me. When I reached my street, I noticed a blacked-out SUV parked across the street. I cautiously kept an eye on them as I gathered my belongings. To my surprise when the doors swung open two familiar bodies stepped out. When I registered who it was, I dropped everything and went sprinting into their arms. *"ACE ANDY!!!!! OH MY GOD HI*!" I screeched with excitement as I embraced them into the tightest hug. "*SURPRISE!*" they said simultaneously as they hugged me back and kissed each side of my face.

We quickly went inside before anyone could possibly see them and call the paparazzi. I put my things away and grabbed some water for them. "*I thought you said you would be coming in soon?*" I said with a surprised tone as I sat across from them. "*Well, we said there was going to be more surprises, so here we are.*" Ace said in a devious tone. "*Plus, we had some time off and yearned for your presence.*" Andy said as he leaned back on the couch. A smile softly crossed my face. "*Well, I appreciate being on your mind and yearning for me. I was planning on cooking some chicken piccata. Do you want to help me?*" I spoke in an innocent tone.

They followed me into the kitchen, and I started to hand the cooking utensils out to them before grabbing the food. I had Ace on my left and Andy on my right. Before I handed off the cutting board to Ace, he held onto one of my hands and placed his hand on the side of my face kissing me softly on the lips. I pulled away smiling. When I handed Andy the mixing bowl, he put his hand on the side of my face and kissed me seductively. I savored the kiss for a minute and pulled away with the largest grin on my face.

I tried to gather my thought process on what all we needed. I turned on some music as we got to work on our dinner. As utensils clinked, laughter wove through my kitchen. The fragrant aroma of all the ingredients coming together brought a sense of happiness and togetherness. We all passed subtle glances to each other as if it was unspoken connections, as we danced to the music playing in the background surges of electrifying emotions danced between us. Andy and I plated up the dishes as Ace washed everything and placed them in the dishwasher. Andy decided to place all 3 of our plates in the oven to stay warm. Before I could ask him as to why he was doing that I could feel Ace running his hand up my arm to the back of my neck, grabbing my hair as he kissed me passionately. Andy's hand roamed my sides, making sure to grab my hips and pull them into his crotch, as he kissed my shoulders and neck. A soft moan escaped my lips. I forgot how good I feel with them.
Ace picked me up and sat me on the kitchen island as Andy unbuttoned my blouse and unsnapped my bra. My breast fell and gently bounced. Ace and Andy's eyes gazed upon my breasts and smiled in delight. They both grabbed one breast each cupping it perfectly in their hands. Their tongues simultaneously licked my nipples and began sucking on them as they worshipped my tender breasts. I moaned in pleasure as they mouth fucked my nipples in tandem. My hands roam their hair as I gently tugged when they gently bit my nipples.

My pussy was becoming drenched and aching for them. I scooted back away from them and unbuttoned and unzipped my pants as I peeled them off. I laid back on the kitchen island spreading my legs as an art display ready for them to feast. Andy rushed his head between my legs slurping up my juices and devouring my pussy. Ace kissed me ferociously. Our tongues danced a hungry tango as he massaged my breast and pinched my nipples between his fingertips. My moans became louder.

73

After I came in Andy's mouth, he switched with Ace and proceeded to kiss me passionately, his tongue deep inside my mouth forcing me to taste the cum I left on his tongue as his fingers became tangled up in my hair. Ace wrapping his arms around my hips forcing me to stay put as I cum all over his face. Ace comes up and pushes me back to lay down on the kitchen island. Andy reaches in his back pocket pulling out two brand new condoms. As they slipped them on, I used my fingers to dance on my clit as they got ready.

Andy was ready first and climbed between my legs with a devilish smile. He slid himself in working my pussy nice and slow warming me up for both massive cocks. Thrusting deeper and faster. My head rolls back in pleasure as Andy rolls his hips into each thrust hitting the holy grail making my back arch in pleasure. My walls start to pulsate harder, and I start to cum again. Andy's eyes roll to the back of his head as his huge hot load explodes into the condom.

Ace switches with Andy and flips me over so I am on my knees. I grab the edge of the island and hold on for dear life as he rams my pussy with his aching cock. With each thrust, Ace's balls slap my clit in the most enticing way. My eyes roll to the back of my head, and I lower my torso to arch my back more. His thrust is getting harder and deeper, but he never leaves my aching pussy. I lean my head back; Andy grabs my throat and starts to squeeze just enough air out of my airway. Ace lets out the loudest moan as he explodes which makes me squirt.

The three of us catch our breath and clean ourselves up. I stopped the guys from getting dressed "*I got freshly fucked by two sexy men, for my birthday can I have a show with my dinner?*" I said in a seductive voice. They looked at me and smiled "*Anything for the most beautiful birthday girl.*" They said simultaneously. So, there we are in the living room. Having our warm chicken piccata dinner naked after an amazing fuck session.

Chapter 13
Concert

This chapter contains:
Profanity
Sexual Assault
Physical Altercations
Threesome

Last night was a dream come true. It was nice sharing laughter, hearing the crazy tour stories, and all the adventures we have shared since they left. I missed Ace and Andy so much; I was excited to see them last night. I was even more thrilled to have my back blown out by them. I hope it can happen at least one more time before they head back out on the road.

I guess I had a pep in my step walking into the office. Because Mindy, Tasha, and Nick watched my every move as I was getting settled in. I was in my own little world dancing and singing to myself. *"I have never seen her like this."* Mindy whispered. *"Well, whatever it is, this needs to happen more often."* Tasha murmured. Nick rolled his eyes *"She got laid."* He said loudly to get my attention. I turned around *"Good morning, and to answer your question, I had a lovely night with Ace and Andy."* My face turned a subtle pink tone as I mentioned their name. Nick shouted, ***"TOLD YOU!"*** I giggled at them as they dispersed like mice trying to find cheese.

I reflected on last night's escapades with a satisfied smile slapped across my face. Seamlessly it transitioned into a productive workday. Several tasks later, I was able to get a minute to myself and send the guys a sweet text message.

Kendra: Hey! Just wanted to let you know that you know how to make an incredible night unforgettable.

Ace: You are the perfect ingredient for an amazing night.

Andy: Can we make it a habit?

Kendra: What if it becomes an addiction?

Ace: I am down for that addiction.

Andy: Who says we are not already addicted?

After reading that text message, I had to put my phone down. A radiant smile stretched across my face with my eyes sparkling with genuine joy, expressing an infectious expression of pure happiness. These guys truly know how to make a woman feel special. I don't want to get my hopes up, but maybe there could be something there for the three of us. Could we pull a long-distance poly relationship off?

Tasha, Nick, and I headed out to the little café nearby for lunch and I kept pondering to myself if this idea could work. *"Are you still thinking about last night?"* asked Nick *"You seem really focused on something."* Tasha mentioned. *"They really know how to make me feel special, kind of thinking about asking them if they want to try a poly relationship."* I said cautiously. Tasha and Nick dropped their forks and looked at each other with surprise before turning their attention towards me. *"Are you **NUTS**?!"* Tasha expressed *"They are rockstars only here for a couple of days."* Nick mentioned. *"I know, I know. I'm crazy! I will just forget about it."* I shut down immediately. Tasha and Nick are correct, they are rock stars here for a break. They are only looking for a good time, not a long time. Plus, I don't know even know one thing about polyamory or the lifestyle.

I stayed a little quiet the rest of the lunch time, I was a bit bummed with their response, but they are correct, I should not get my hopes up for a fantasy lifestyle. I need to stay focused and only allow some fun into my life. It is a lot safer to not get attached. From Dimitri trying to kill me all the way to Lily being killed. Being alone and single is going to be the safest route for me.

We headed back to the office and my pep step calmed down after I came back to reality. Mindy went to pick up her children from school since the babysitter's car was in the shop. I slumped into my chair to get back to work when my phone chimed.

Andy: Hey! Sorry we have been in rehearsal all day. Wanted to let you know you have VIP access to the concert this weekend.

Ace: It is our gift to you for your birthday. We will drop it off tomorrow.

Kendra: Guys! You spoil me so much! Thank you!

Even though Tasha and Nick brought me back to reality. It doesn't hurt to live in a little daydream just until my birthday is over, right?

The next couple of days passed. Ace and Andy swung by the office to drop off the tickets to their show before heading to the final rehearsal. When they walked into my office, they each had a balloon, bouquet of beautiful flowers, my favorite candy, and a bottle of wine that we shared the first time we had dinner, and two jewelry boxes. One was a pair of diamond earrings and the other one was a diamond rose necklace. My mouth dropped when I saw everything and gave them the longest hug and kissed them sweetly on the lips. *"You guys did not need to do this, thank you so much for making me feel special."* I expressed my gratitude towards them both feeling like the luckiest woman in the world. *"You deserve the world Kendra,"* said Ace. *"We wanted to be the ones to make you feel special for your birthday."* Andy mentioned. My head swirled into dreamland as I was lost in a vivid reverie, living in lavish scenes and scenarios of us as a polyamorous relationship. Oh, such a lovely temporary escape into a world of endless possibilities.

The night of the concert is here. Nick and Tasha are going to meet me there. I am staring at myself in the mirror. I think Ace and Andy will love my outfit. I looked at my thigh high boots and slowly brought my gaze up to my waist. I dressed in crotchless laced panties and black mini leather skirt, up past my belly button laid a see-through mesh crop top with my breast freely bouncing, my nipples covered in black X pasties.

My neck and ears were decorated with the beautiful jewelry they gave me. The final touches were a couple squirts of my new perfume. It was a captivating blend of jasmine and vanilla with subtle notes of amber and musk. It was certainly a sensuous and alluring aroma to make Ace and Andy drop to their knees and not forget about me.

We made our way to the bar as the guest stars took the stage. As we got into the mood and enjoyed the sets before the guys took the stage. We started to go into full celebration mode. From dancing, to taking shots, and pictures we certainly had a blast. But things quickly turned dark. Right before Ace and Andy took the stage. A creep had his eye on me. I was slightly bent over on the table when out of no were a giant forceful hand smacked and grabbed my ass barely touching the outline of my pussy. My mouth dropped to the ground after feeling violated. I slammed my shot glass down and turned around. This man stood well over six feet tall. I looked him up and down in silence. *"Never been handled by man before pretty little thing."* The disgusting disgrace of a human said. I rolled my eyes before grabbing his neck and forcefully squeezing away his air, making him drop to his knees. *"Looks like someone has never been handled before."* I squeezed his neck harder removing all the air from him as I stared at him as his body squirmed crying for oxygen. Once his body collapsed, I called security over and told them what happened. Tasha and Nick were too stunned to speak and just went with the flow. As the paramedics dragged the guy off, we celebrated with one last shot before making our way towards the stage.

As the guys took the stage, a pulsating sea of energy as the crowd swayed to the rhythmic beats of their music, the vibrant beaming lights illuminated the stage making everything come to life. Ace and Andy poured their heart and soul into the show. The surrounding air was charged with excitement as they rocked the stage. Towards the end of the show Ace gave the security guard a signal and he came towards me. *"You're going to need to come with me."* The security guard yelled towards me. I looked back at Nick and Tasha, and they waved goodbye to me as they finished watching the show. The security guard guided me towards the dressing room of Ace and Andy. He unlocked the door and let me get settled in.

I scanned the room and saw every little detail about them they had left in there. These guys are something else. Roughly 20 minutes later they came into the dressing room drenched in sweat. Andy ran up to me, picking me up and kissing me passionately against the wall. *"You look fucking sexy baby."* He whispered in my ear as he attacked my neck in kisses and nibbles. *"My turn Andy."* Ace declared. Andy stepped aside and grabbed my hips firmly, staring deep into my eyes *"You look and smell divine."* Ace said in a low growl. Our lips exchange an electrifying kiss. *"How horny are my two sexy men?"* I asked seductively. *"My cock has been throbbing since I saw you on stage."* Ace said with a chuckle. *"All set I wanted to fuck you on stage."* Andy mentioned. I smiled deviously. Before leaning over the arm of the couch hiking up my skirt to expose the crotchless entrance to my men.

Behind me I can hear them unzipping their pants, quiet moans of *"Oh fuck baby"* can be heard from them both. Ace quickly spits on his rock-hard cock and slides it in nice and slow feeling me on every inch. I let out a moan before I motion Andy over to suck on his aching cock while Ace enjoys my pussy. Andy moans as his head falls back while fucking my mouth. As I start to cum from Ace pounding my tight little pussy. He slaps my ass as Andy's cock is deep into my throat. The first cum session was not enough. They needed to cum one more time. They switch. Andy makes his cock right at home and fingers my clit as he thrusts deep inside making me pulsate around his massive cock. Ace holds my face with both hands placed delicately as he slowly fucks my mouth, moving his massive cock from tip to base nice and slow. We all three cum simultaneously. We all collapsed in pure ecstasy and bliss from pleasure.

Chapter 14
Skate Night

This chapter contains:
Nervousness
Excitement

I was still buzzing from last night's concert and dressing room fun. The music still echoing through my mind and my body remembers Ace and Andy's throbbing cock exploding. I laid in my bed reminiscing about the rhythm that lingers in my veins and pleasure both give me.

Part of me yearned to know if the feelings they had towards me could be more than just random hook ups when they are in town, or if I was just seen as a rand-ho. The chemistry we all share together is mind blowing and comforting at the same time. I laid there going deeper and deeper down a rabbit hole of us possibly being in a polyamorous relationship, and the fact that I have possibly gone psycho from being single. I don't know how long I was deep in my thoughts. But my phone chimed with Ace and Andy ringtones.

Ace: Good morning, beautiful!

Andy: Good morning darling!

I snapped out of my thoughts when I heard their ring tone. A smile crossed my face, the thoughts that had my mind twisted in a bunch dispersed and relaxed.

Kendra: Good morning fellas.

Ace: Hope you had fun. I know I did.

Andy: I know I had a blast.

Kendra: I did have fun. Thank you for making my birthday fun.

Ace: Anything for you!

Andy: You're welcome!

Kendra: Can I ask a question?

Ace: Shoot

Andy: What's up?

Kendra: Umm…. Do you like me for something more than hooking up or do you want to keep it strictly hook ups. I know it is early and it has been fun. I just need clarification.

I took a deep breath as I waited for their response. But I needed to know what was happening between us. My heart was rushing as I waited for their response.

Ace: I have a huge crush on you, but with the schedule we have. We are stuck.

Andy: I would love to call you mine. But the schedule doesn't allow us to have a personal life much.

I stared at their response and my heart broke into a million pieces as I read between the lines. I was only good enough to be a hook up not a first choice. Thankfully, I was able to hide my pain with text.

Kendra: Ok, I just wanted to make sure. I have a busy day ahead. Thank you for my birthday again, I really appreciate it.

They read the message I sent but did not respond. I probably screwed up whatever we had going on. It did put me in a funk knowing I was nothing more than just a piece of ass. Trying to find love in the city of sin has been a challenge for sure. The day seemed to drag on after our short awkward conversation. I know I was not going to see the guys after today, they are going on another international tour soon.

When bedtime arrived, I couldn't have been happier. I could sleep away today. Monday is tomorrow and I can bombard myself with work and ignore the thoughts in my head.

When walking into the office I saw Nick being cheerful like he was going to burst from excitement. *"What has you cheery?"* I asked cautiously. *"I have a plan for this weekend! The ice rink is having an adult only night."* Nick said gleefully. I haven't been ice skating in years. But he really wanted to go. *"Sounds like fun, I could use the distraction."* I answered. He scurried off happily as he was excited that I agreed to this fun time. I am sure Tasha will be down to go as well.

I got to work drafting several documents, managing case files that had court this week, contacting clients for finishing touches on their cases. The day flew by as I was knee deep in the work in front of me. It was nice to focus on work, it was a break from my thoughts. Living in a fantasy of a possible relationship with Ace and Andy had me losing control. I was slowly slipping into a dark place, and I did not want to go through that again. Skating will be good for my mental health. Hopefully, it pulls me out of this funk.

The week passed quickly and before I knew it, Friday was here. Nick shared the details of the party in our group chat. Tasha was nervous because she had never been ice skating before. I on the other hand I know I will be rusty.

After work I put some relaxing music on and did some yoga to get my body ready to be on the ice. I sat on my yoga mat and closed my eyes. As the gentle instrumental music gracefully plays in the background. I synchronize my breathing to the soothing rhythms. While flowing through the movements, I feel as if I can hear Lily guiding me. I can smell lavender surrounding me in an embracing hug. I let out a soft sigh as I open my eyes and a single tear falls down my face. I softly whispered out loud *"I miss you so much Lily."* Cold chills danced down my shoulders to my fingertips. Wiping the teardrop that was on my cheek, I softly smiled. I know she is close by.

I savored the moment just a little bit longer before it was time to get ready. Walking into my spare bedroom closet, I reached for my gear of warm thermals, leggings, knit hat, long sleeves, and skates. I hurried downstairs and into the car and took off towards the ice rink.

Pulling up to the rink I can see Nick and Tasha outside by the front doors. I parked the car and before opening my car door another car pulled up beside me. I got out before anyone could have gotten out of the passenger side. But when I turned around to lock the car after grabbing my bag a tall masculine man with a large build got my attention. He had long hair tied back into a bun and a scruffy beard. Walking towards Nick and Tasha, I could feel him watching my every move. It sent a chill down my spine as it reminded me of when Dimitri watched me like his lion ready to pounce on his prey.

We checked in and paid while this giant of a man walked up beside us and said, *"Hey Astrid."* making the woman behind the desk blush as she let him in without hesitation. We looked at Astrid and I asked, *"So Astrid, who is he?"* Astrid who already took off into dreamland let out a sigh *"Only the hottest most single assistant coach of the hockey team."* Nick, Tasha, and I just stared at each other as drool started to fall from Astrid's mouth. We giggled and walked in the rink area, scanning the area we found a perfect little clearing along the benches.

Shockingly there was a good amount of people here to skate. As the lights went low and music started to bump. I tied my skates up and got my bearings before stepping on to the ice. As I turned to help Tasha on to the ice, I felt a pair of giant hands holding onto my waist and a low husky voice say, *"Sorry love, need to step out excuse me."* I froze in place as I stumbled for my words *"Sorry, newbie!"* I was too nervous to make eye contact with him. Tasha just looked at me dumb founded as I completely fumbled the move this man just put on me. He moved us out of the way with ease and skated out into the rink. Tasha was losing her balance, so I had to quickly shift my attention back onto her and get her taken care of showing her how to skate. After two laps she got the hang of being on the ice but still took it easy.

I ended up forgetting about the assistant coach while skating. I was in my happy place and started to feel confident enough to try some old tricks. I couldn't go crazy as there were others on the ice. But I did want to do to a spin, it was always a high for me. I took in a deep breath of the crisp air and let out a sigh as I stood in the middle of the ice rink preparing myself to spin. The ice welcomed me back with each stride and the thrill coursed through my veins. The memory of the spins and twirls came flooding back. With a deep breath, I gathered more momentum, positioned my arms, my heart pounding I initiated the spin microseconds before a drunk skater bumped into me, knocking me off balance.

Shockingly the assistant coach was a knight in shining armor. Catching me in mid fall pulling me into his rock-hard chest as he spun me into a safe landing. Both of us panting heavily as we came down from the thrill. I smiled and grabbed his shirt as I stared at his lips, they were full and soft, and he had a perfect smile. *"Thank you for saving me."* I said leaning into him. He smiled as his hands gripped my waist a little longer than anticipated. A sly smile crossed his face, he tucked a strand of my hair behind my ear before saying *"Anything for you love."* We stared deep into each other's eyes for what felt like an eternity. I stood up and fixed myself *"Thank you again, I appreciate it, I am Kendra."* My voice was slightly shaky. He chuckled *"It is no problem love, name is Ryker."* I got called away before we could say anything else to each other. I waved goodbye as my cheeks turned a pink tone from blushing so hard.

I skated over to Nick and Tasha to see what was wrong. Turned out Tasha twisted her ankle when getting out of the ice rink. Apparently, she slipped on the poly threshold, I did that in my earlier skating days, talk about being the slipperiest part of the rink. That is worse than slipping on water. I rushed to the front desk to get an ice pack, but she said it was near the dressing room. I rushed over to the dressing room and spotted the first aid kit in the hallway. Closing the first aid kit I hear *"**Kendra!**"*

Turning around I see Ryker running up towards me. *"What's up Ryker?"* he smiled and stumbled with his words *"The rink will be closed tomorrow for maintenance and with what happened, you looked like you needed ice time, do you want to come here tomorrow with me?"* Shifting my weight side to side I nervously asked, *"Like a date?"* Ryker ran his fingers over his head and blushed *"It can be."* I smiled and pulled his shirt down towards me to get closer to his ear *"Sounds perfect see you tomorrow."* I whispered giving him a soft kiss on the cheek. Like any attorney, I had a card in my pocket and pulled it out slipping it into his pocket. I grabbed the ice pack and made my way to Nick and Tasha.

Breaking the ice pack to get it ready, Tasha's ankle was swollen terribly. We got some ice on it and got her out to the car, Nick was taking her home since she caught a ride with him.

I got in my car looking in the review mirror seeing the rink, I smiled from ear to ear. *"I will see you tomorrow."* I said almost squealing.

Chapter 15
Zamboni

This chapter contains:

Profanity
Vehicle play

Standing in my closet I started to panic. I didn't have anything to wear for my date in a couple hours. I was internally panicking. I wanted to look sexy for this date, but it is in an ice rink. I didn't have any of my costumes from my competition days and that would just be too much. I threw myself on to the bed in defeat. I had to accept my fate and wear other workout clothes. Maybe this date will be innocent? I thought to myself. I rolled myself off the bed and got dressed. My confidence certainly took a hit, I did not like how I was looking for this date. I had to remember; Ryker literally saved me when I was a sweaty mess.

I let out an aggravated sigh as I made my way to the car. I put on some music to cheer up my spirits as I drove across town to the rink. The parking lot was bare, the only car in the parking lot besides mine was Rykers. My nerves decided to go havoc and my stomach twisted up in knots. Why am I so nervous? I took a couple of deep breaths and popped an anti-nausea pill just in case to calm my stomach down. I took one last breath before heading inside.

Walking inside the rink was nerve wracking compared to the other day. A rink that was so lively and loud to cold and quiet. It felt eerie being inside and being the only one in there. I looked around and headed towards the ice. Searching for Ryker. I peeked my head nervously through the door and called out *"Ryker? It's me Kendra…."* I waited for a response before going inside and closing the door. Nothing, it was pure silence. I waited for a couple more minutes before calling out again even louder. *"RYKER? IT'S ME KENDRA!"* Before turning around and leaving I hear *"KENDRA WAIT! I apologize love. I was in the back gathering some stuff for our date and I didn't hear you come in.*" Ryker calls out as he runs towards me. He reached out his hand for me to grab to follow him. He took my bag as we walked towards the bench area.

We approached the bench area dressed in blankets and pillows, to set up a cozy picnic area. I smiled when I saw the effort Ryker put into this date. I smiled as my eyes scanned over the view and saw that he put together a charcuterie board and various snacks from salty to sweet and a bottle of Pinot Noir, battery operated candles and a bouquet of tulips and roses. I gently squeezed Ryker's hand and leaned into his side "*This is beautiful Ryker.*" Ryker smiled and wrapped his arm around my side "*I wanted to make our first date special.*" I felt my heart flutter for the first time since leaving my ex.

A couple of hours passed as we talked and snacked, we shared laughs and gentle kisses. It was perfect. We decided to put on our skates and take to the ice. We warmed up with a couple of lazy laps hand in hand. I skated away and went to do my own thing. I glided effortlessly across the glistening ice. Carving an elegant path, tracing delicate narratives on the ice as I gained momentum. I extended my arms then brought them close to my body tucking in to lift off the ice and spin gracefully landing on my back leg. I smiled as I stuck that landing. The thrill and excitement that filled my heart brought back memories of a good time in my life.

When I turned around, I could see Ryker clapping since he didn't have to save me from falling, and that I knew what I was doing as a skater. I skated up to him and wrapped my arms around his neck and gently pulled him down into a sweet kiss. His arms wrapped around my waist and as he deepened the kiss. Our tongues started to play with each other, teasing each other. Ryker's hand moves up my back to the back of my head holding me close as our kiss turns passionate. He pulls away and rests his forehead against mine. We both smile at each other as we catch our breath.

An hour later we took a break from skating since it was getting late, we needed to clean up the ice and picnic area. Ryker disappeared before coming back out on the Zamboni. "*Wanna go for a ride?*" he asks. I smiled as he helped me up into the seat. *"I have always wanted to drive one of these."* I mentioned. He pulled me onto his lap, as I circled my hips into a more comfortable position, Ryker's gripped tightened around my hips as his breath hitches in his throat.

The Devil on my shoulder jumped for joy for my bold move. I decided to twist my hips seductively teasing him as I drove the Zamboni. Ryker softly moaned *"Oh fuck."* He reached down and pressed a button to put on auto pilot. He adjusted his lap and I decided to grind nice and slow on his growing cock. I spun around and kissed his thick full lips passionately as my hips twisted on him. Ryker's hands roamed my body pulling me down to put more weight on his cock. His breath was heavy.

I got onto my knees and helped Ryker pull his sweats. His cock had girth; it took both hands to wrap around it. I massaged him up and down, I leaned down and dragged my tongue from the base to the tip as I looked deep into his eyes. I enveloped his hung cock deep into my mouth bobbing my head up and down nice and slow. I massaged his cock with my tongue as his head fell back in pleasure. Ryker held my head down as I gagged a bit on his hung cock. He pulled me up and kissed me passionately as he pulled my leggings off. I positioned myself on his lap as I teased his tip at my entrance. Kissing his neck and earlobe ever so gently as I grind my clit on his tip.

Ryker growled and bit his lower lip as he stared at my tits after pulling my shirt up. He shoved himself deep inside making me scream in pleasure, feeling him thrust himself under me. I match my hips to his rhythm. Ryker's hand roams up my back to my shoulders and pushes me down even deeper. My head rolled back as I started to scream in pleasure as his cock twitched inside my pulsating pussy. His lips traced down from my jaw to my chest. One of Ryker's hands shoved up my shirt and sports bra as he sucked on my nipples. I started to cum all over him. He felt me cum and lost control. He put me against the steering wheel and held onto the Zamboni as he fucked me hard on the steering wheel. I lost control of my body as it convulses in pleasure. I squirted all over Ryker as he exploded multiple times. The Zamboni came to a screeching stop as we caught our breath and smiled at each other.

"That was amazing." Ryker said as he caught his breath smiling at me. *"I agree."* I said as I fixed my clothes. We finished getting dressed and cleaning up. Before we walked out of the ice rink. Ryker pinned me to the wall grabbing my throat in a loving touch as he kissed me passionately one last time before leaving. *"I need to see you again love. Please don't make me beg to take more of your time."* Ryker said. I smiled and held his hand that was around my throat as I gave him puppy eyes *"Then do not make me wait."* I said. Ryker smiled and kissed me one last time with one hand tangled in my hair and the other wrapped around my waist. The passion between us grew as if we were meant to be. Our make out session lasted for a while. I wanted to fuck him again as the burning desire grew between us.

Ryker kissed my neck and pulled away *"I will be good but fuck I need you again."* I smiled and leaned against the wall *"Guess we will need more time together soon."* We didn't want to leave each other as it took forever to leave each other's embrace. Standing at our cars, we held on to each other talking about our next date. I felt at home in his embrace. There was so much we had in common, our energy and connections flowed with ease. I thanked the big man up in the sky for our paths crossing. If it was not for Ryker saving me the other day. I would not be feeling this happy in the moment. We finally said good night to each other and went our separate ways home.

Driving home I felt happiness, something I have not felt since meeting Lily. Maybe it was a sign that it was ok to move on and make memories with someone new. I was excited to see where things go with Ryker.

Chapter 16
Bummer

This chapter contains

Self-Play

Days passed since I last seen Ryker, I was busy at the office preparing for court for my client. Even though we did not get to have time together or we did not text, we would be on the phone talking into the late hours. I was amazed by his goals and ambitions. Ryker's dreams were wild and achievable all at the same time.

Our connection grew immensely, but at the same time I was hesitant. I was not very lucky in the love department. Plus, learning about Ryker, he made it clear he was waiting to be recruited by the National Hockey League. I would never be the person who held someone back from their dream, he has worked so hard and if the opportunity comes knocking at his door. I want him to chase after it.

When the weekend finally arrived, my heart filled with enjoyment. Because it meant that Ryker was going to come over for dinner and a movie. I hurried off to the store to grab a few things for dinner and movie snacks. Passing down the aisle where I met Lily is still a challenge to go down. But I suck it up and head down where I became covered in cold chills. I quickly grabbed what was needed and walked towards the register to pay.

Getting home I threw everything on the kitchen island and got to work to marinate the salmon and started making the tiramisu for dessert. When I set the tiramisu in the fridge to get cold my phone chimed.

Ryker: Hey Kendra! I am sorry but I can't make it tonight.

My heart sank a bit reading his text message. I was disappointed that he was not able to follow through with our plans. But I understood that things happen. I replied.

Kendra: Aww that's a bummer. But I can understand.

Ryker: I was informed an NHL recruiter will be at the game Friday. Gotta buckle down.

Kendra: That's amazing! I am so EXCITED for you!!!

Ryker: Thank you! Again, I am terribly sorry.

Kendra: Do not be sorry for following your dreams.

I leaned against the counter and poured some whiskey and started to cook the salmon, rice pilaf, and asparagus. Reaching into the cabinet I grabbed some containers to store the leftovers in. I was bummed because the plans fell through. Hell, if I was being honest with myself; finding love in a tourist roundabout city felt like it was going to be damn near impossible. What the fuck do I have to do to get more than just a couple of hook ups. I decided to end the night early and take a warm relaxing bubble bath.

The tingling sensation between my legs was not going anywhere. I grabbed my vibrator and turned on the warm water. I poured my favorite bubble bath soap and added a couple drops of body oil. Slowly slipping into the warm tempered water until enveloping me. The aroma of the fragrant bubbles gently rising to my nose. My muscles unwind and sink further into the calming ambiance.

I toyed with the vibrator between my hands finding the perfect vibration to play with. The third setting is the solid BUZZ my aching clit was needing. Sliding the vibrator into the water started a ripple effect which enlightened me. I ran the toy across my nipples which made my breathing heavier. My nipples became engorged as the vibrator danced around my areolas. I slowly dragged the vibrator down my stomach and rubbed my lips as my legs parted. My head falls back enjoying the sensations between my legs as I slide the vibrator in and out. My breathing becomes labored as my eyes start to roll backwards as the building of the climax grows more and more. My heart racing as I rub the vibrator ferociously against my clit faster and faster until I explode. My body convulsing in pleasure splashing water outside of the tub. I laid there in the water until the water turned cold. Granted it was nothing like what I imagined the night could have been, but it was something to take care of the tingling urges my body was craving.

Chapter 17
Chance of a lifetime

This chapter contains:

Public Sex

Court was comical throughout the week. I honestly could have never imagined a Las Vegas court system to be this easy. Friday evening rolled around, and it was time to go. As I made my way out of the courthouse, I had to swing by the house to change. I knew it was going to be a big night for Ryker and I wanted to show my spirit by being there and supporting him.

Arriving at the skating rink the parking lot was packed with cars and people excited about the game and walking into the rink. I didn't want to make Ryker nervous by letting him know I was here. So, I sat in the upper bleachers making myself blend into the crowd. I sent Ryker a quick text message.

Kendra: Good luck tonight! You got this!

Ryker: Thanks love!

I didn't want to bug him as Ryker needed to keep his focus on the game. I noticed the recruits who sat closest to the rink jotting notes down in their notepads. Once the puck dropped the thrilling show began with each team engaging in the plays they practiced countless times as they sprinted on the ice for each play. The crowd roars with excitement as each team executes the skills they have been practicing. The feeling of achievement came out of them. The tension builds between the players and the crowds as they get closer to the goals. Ryker's strongest player executed the perfect slapshot soaring the puck into the net. The arena erupts into celebratory cheers, tears, high fives, and body bumps. The teams displayed perfect sportsmanship. Ryker's team triumphantly skates into the spotlight to engage with the crowd for their historical win.

I sat back and waited as the people disperse on their way. Watching the recruits talk and heading towards the locker rooms to talk to Ryker. I knew he had this position in the bag. I waited until it was my turn to congratulate him. Looking out onto the ice and the perfect date we had. I am bummed that our time together will be cut short. But the National Hockey League needs an amazing coach like Ryker. He also deserves this lifelong goal of his. An hour passes by, and the recruits headed out. I took a deep breath before I congratulated Ryker. Soaking in the arena knowing it will probably be the last time I step foot in here.

Quietly stepping into the empty locker room, I knock on his office door before walking inside. Ryker comes sprinting up to me picking up me and spinning us around in a full circle as he plants the most passionate filled kiss on my lips. I pulled away and asked, *"You got the job?"* Ryker was filled with excitement smiling ear to ear *"Yes, I did! You are looking at the new assistant coach for the Boston Bruins!"* I squeezed Ryker in the tightest hug with excitement but deep down it was our final hug. *"Eek! I am so happy for you!"* I squealed.

Ryker embraced me in the tightest hug and stared deeply into my eyes. His fingers slowly traced my jawline to my chin lifting my face up. He leaned in towards my face and our lips met for a slow passionate burning kiss. His hands roamed my body as they pulled me closer to him. As the burning desire grows our lip lock turned into a starving deprived touch. Attacking the sensitive areas of our neck and jawlines the tingling sensation between my legs grew more and more. I start ripping off Rykers clothes as he started to rip off mine. *"I need you, Kendra."* Ryker whispers in my ear. *"Take me."* I whispered back. A devilish grin arises from Rykers lips. Ryker picked me up effortlessly and rubbed his tip against my lips until my lips were wet enough for him to easily slip inside. Pumping in a pleasurable rhythm making me moan sweet sounds into Rykers ear. His breath becomes animalistic, and his hands grip my ass tighter. He opened the office door and slams my back against the cold locker pinning our hands above our heads as he rams his ribbed cock deeper inside me. The screams of pleasure between us echo throughout the locker room. Climax after climax Ryker then moves us to the showers.

Turning the hot water on the steam fills the area. The cold tiles press against my back makes my back arch involuntarily making my pussy pulsate over Rykers cock making him explode deep inside. The sensational waves flooded over us, and a new side came out to play an animal was released from Ryker as the water soaked us. The thrusts become rapid as sweat from our bodies and water mix. Ryker clamps his jaw onto my shoulder as he tries to hush his whimpers of pleasure. Cuming repeatedly until we felt lifeless. We slid down to the shower floor with me resting my head on his shoulder facing him. I cup his face and give him a sweet kiss on his lips *"I am so proud of you for following your dream and achieving it."* Ryker smiled *"This is the chance of a lifetime. Thank you."* We sat there in silence until the water turned cold.

After getting dressed, Ryker walked me out to the car and kissed me tenderly knowing this was possibly the last time we would see each other again.

Chapter 18
See you later

This chapter contains:
Abandonment

A couple of days passed and there was no word from Ryker. I know he had a lot to do before leaving for Boston and what we had was only momentary. I tried not to get completely heartbroken as dating and finding love in Las Vegas has been damn near impossible. I shifted my focus to another case. With my text messages being ignored I had to drown myself in work to not feel completely heartbroken. Tasha and Nick walked by the office to check on me since I have been keeping my distance. *"Knock, knock"* they said simultaneously. I looked up from my stack of files I was preparing for court later this month. *"Hey!"* I said as I scrambled to clean everything up to shift my focus to them. *"Everything ok? You haven't said much since the whole Ryker incident"* Tasha mentioned. *"Seems like someone is grieving over a broken heart pretty bad."* Nick chimed in. I played with my fingers as I fought back my emotions. *"I am fine, just trying to get the next case in order."* My words stumble out of my mouth. I know they are on to the game I am trying to play.

Tasha came around my desk and hugged me while Nick announced, *"There is an event this weekend that we can check out in the art district."* Tasha and I looked at Nick and shook our heads in agreement to go check it out.

While I buried myself in work, I felt myself slump to shame as the text messages I send to Ryker are completely ignored. I don't know if he is busy or ghosted me. Deep down I was feeling ghosted. I started to feel like I was disposable and only good for one thing- sex.

I had to get out of this slump, shopping therapy was calling my name. I leaned back and tapped my chin with my finger. I was trying to think of what could possibly buy. Should it be a couple of outfits, some skin care, or a designer bag. I dabbled for a while on what to get. Tasha walked by and made a quick stop and stared at me to study my demeanor. *"Everything ok?"* Tasha asked as she leaned in my door frame. I got out of my trance shaking my head back into reality *"Yeah, shopping therapy is calling my name since I am in a slump with Ryker leaving."* I answered. Tasha walked in sitting down with her mom advice mode activated *"I know finding love in Las Vegas is difficult especially with hook up culture practically taking over, everything is overlooked and there is no way out. You know he was heading to the pros and there was nothing we could do about Lily. Maybe, try focusing on you for a bit."* Tasha suggested.

Hearing her speak about Lily felt like a wound being reopened. Before jumping into defense mode, I knew it was necessary and out of love. *"You're right Tasha, although I would love to do some retail therapy, I think I need a break from the entire dating scene and give myself a detox, I have not had the best of luck."* I say in a cogent tone. A soft confident smile crossed Tasha's lips before her sassiness took over. *"Retail therapy is the best method for a restart though. Shopping at the Square this weekend. Sound good?"* Tasha said with enthusiasm. I laughed and shook my head in agreement. She saw Nick in the hallway and told him about the shopping trip this weekend and he was stoked.

Since shopping was now in place for this weekend. I got back to work. Several hours passed and I got a measly couple of work items completed. My thoughts trickled back to Ryker, maybe I should go to the rink tonight in the off chance he is there. I know it was probably a bad idea. But I wanted closure, I felt like I deserve that especially without connection. At the end of the day, I headed towards the rink. By the time I got to the parking lot of the rink, the overwhelming sensation of this is a bad idea flooded my mind. There were a couple of cars parked, but Ryker's car was nowhere to be seen. I took a deep breath and threw my head back against the head of the seat. I lost my chance, he is gone.

A deep sigh left my mouth letting my soul feel defeated. I started the car and made my way home to start the recovery process from another broken heart. On the way home, I stopped by the liquor store and picked up a bottle of Johnnie Walker Blue Label, a good burn to the rage I feel deep down.

I got home and poured a glass of Johnny Walker on the rocks while I started to make a roasted salmon risotto. The aromas of a delicious meal filled my heart with happiness. Being a simple woman has its advantages. Yummy food and a delicious drink certainly turned my night around. The burn from the scotch helped ease the feeling of abandonment. I looked at our conversations one last time and concluded that Ryker left for good.

Chapter 19
Unwanted

This chapter contains:
Flash backs
PTSD
Night Terrors

You know the eerie sensation you get when the day is bad? I woke with a feeling that something today would not be good. Could it have been a possible car accident today or running into someone you dread. That was how I felt as I got ready to go shopping with the gang. As much as I tried to ignore the silent screams from my guardian angels, I fought against it and went about my day anyways. My chest weighed heavy, and my movement was slow. Spiritually it felt as if my body was walking to its death bed. The overwhelming feeling of staying home was practically screaming so loud that I could not hear anything around me. As I made my way to my car the battery was dead. I sent a quick text message to the gang.

Kendra: Looks like my guardians do not want me to leave. My car battery is dead. Anyone want to pick me up?

Tasha: Only if you buy me cinnamon sugar pretzel bites.

Nick: Ooh those do sound delicious.

Kendra: Deal.

Tasha arrives shortly after, and we take off to the Square to do some much needed retail therapy. Nick meets us outside the pretzel shop, and I treat us to some pretzel bites. Because shopping on an empty stomach is a terrible idea. Once our stomach was full, we made our way from shop-to-shop window shopping and purchasing what caught our eyes. Escaping from the stress of the world and work. It was nice enjoying life. I tried on several outfits, shoes, and checked out new purses and sunglasses. We passed a new store that just recently opened, and it had elegant ball gowns. When we walked in, we were greeted wall to wall with beautiful shades and textures of flowy gowns that sparkled perfectly as the sun shone through the windows. It was like being inside a disco ball.

Tasha and I gasped as we walked through the store. I stumbled across this elegant, red, satin dress with a feathered corset with diamonds sewn all around and down the skirt of the dress. My jaw dropped when I laid my eyes upon it. *"You should try it on."* Tasha nudges me with her encouraging voice. *"It's beautiful! I would have nowhere to wear it."* I said in a discouraging tone. *"This would be perfect for the charity ball later this year."* Tasha mentions. I took a deep breath and let out a quick sigh. *"Alright!"* I waved over to an associate and made my way to the dressing room. I slipped it on, and it fit like a glove. I was impressed that it fit perfectly.

I stepped out of the dressing room and made my way towards Tasha and Nick to look at myself in the mirror. I saw their reactions before seeing my reflection. Their jaw dropped and I could see a tear in Tasha's eyes. I turned and felt like royalty with what I saw in the mirror. The world around me disappeared as I fell in love with what I saw in the mirror. Even if I never wear this dress in public, I can wear it to boost my confidence. I never felt more beautiful than I did in this dress.

Time seemed to pass as I admired what I saw, I tossed around the idea of purchasing it. When the sales associate snapped me out of my daydream to see if I was going to purchase or not. I had to make a rush decision and of course, I agreed to purchase it. My retail therapy was complete. I was on cloud nine of dopamine as soon as my fingers wrapped around the straps of the bag that contained the most beautiful dress I have ever owned.

After finishing up with retail therapy and lunch Tasha and I made our way back to my house. As I pulled up the mailman walked up to hand me a letter. I thanked him and looked at the letter that was addressed to me with no sender information. I stared long and hard at it. Tasha intercepted my thoughts *"Who is it from?"* I looked up at her *"There is no sender information?"* I answered as a wave of uncertainty rushed through my body and I started to shake uncontrollably from being nervous. I asked Tasha to come in with me. I dropped the bags on the kitchen island and stared at the unknown letter.

A high pitch in my left ear almost deafens me and makes my knees buckle. My guardians are trying to send me a message as I hold this letter. I take a deep breath and quickly open the letter. Tasha stands there with moral support as I scan the handwriting of a creepy letter from an unknown person. My heart rate increases and tremors start to take over as I read each word. I become lightheaded and short of breath as I get closer to the end. I fall to the floor in a panic attack hyper ventilating as I see the signature of this disturbing letter. Tasha dropped to her knees and enveloped me in a tight hug to make me focus on getting my breathing under control. Before she could get a word out, I handed her the letter for her to read.

Kendra,

It has been some time since I have put my hands on you. Let alone my throbbing cock in your pussy to declare you as mine. Sitting in these cell walls away from you, not able to watch your every move. Not able to see you sleeping is driving me insane. I want to smell your hair; I can still feel it wrapped between my fingers from when I dragged you by your hair that night. Seeing you bleeding on the floor still brings a smile to my face. When I get out, it will be my life mission to find you and finish out what I did not finish. I cannot wait to fuck your bleeding dead corps.

This will not be the last that you hear from me. I hope to consume your endless thoughts.

-Dimitri

"What the ACTUAL FUCK!" screamed Tasha as she sprinted to my printer to make several copies to send to the authorities. My thoughts drifted back to that night when

Dimitri attacked me. I thought I was safe, I thought he was gone forever. Now it is his life mission to hunt me down like prey and finish the job? What the fuck did I get myself into? I loved my life in Vegas. It took forever to get comfortable in my house again. I started to relive the night and started to sweat and lose control of my breathing as I felt warm and wet all over my torso. It felt like the wounds opened and I was bleeding out again.

Tasha was rushing around trying to find my medication and calling my therapist for an emergency session. She couldn't get my attention away from me patting my body as I checked for bleeding. So, she took matters into her own hands and shoved two pills into my mouth and forced me to drink some water. My therapist was on speaker, Tasha informed her of what happened. I was on the brink of completely slipping away until the medication kicked in. We talked for an hour until I felt at ease, Tasha finally made her way home.

By nighttime, I was not tired enough to sleep. My thoughts were drowning me in waves. He knows my home and the memories of what he did to me. I thought I had suppressed the memories of that night deep down, but Dimitri's letter ripped that scab off with ease. Sitting in my bed my mind rushed to how he watched me sleep. How did he get in, when did he get in? Hours passed; my body finally crashed into a deep sleep. Visions of every encounter I had with Dimitri replayed on endless repeat.

I tossed and turned all night, not an ounce of rest was earned. I felt defeated and exhausted. I made so much stride in winning my life back from that beast, that one letter ripped it all away from me. I had to come up with a plan to restart my life over in Vegas. I was not letting him control me or my life from behind the prison walls. I knew what needed to be done.

Luckily with the inheritance I had enough to put a down payment. Thankfully I have been blessed with enough to take actions into my own hands and I had to make some necessary changes to what I was going to do with the inheritance. I started to look up homes for sale in armed and gated communities, sent an email to my attorney with an attachment of Dimitri's letter, started researching the best states to get an anonymous LLC, and lastly sent an email to my realtor to give them a heads up that I will be on the market soon and a list of addresses I would like to tour.

I was not expecting to hear back from anyone until Monday. The feeling of defeat was disappearing as I was gaining traction on bettering my life and feeling safe with a new outcome.

Chapter 20

A Double Surprise

This Chapter Contains:

Pregnancy Announcement

Monday rolled around and my emails filled with responses and accepting google calendar dates for touring new homes. I quickly filled out the documents for my anonymous LLC. I will be damned if I ever let this pathetic piece of shit control my life. I was going to make him my bitch without him knowing it. My attorney informed me that he was being taken into solitary confinement for contacting me. The feeling of winning was outweighing the trauma he put me though.

The week came and went. I noticed Tasha was not at work as much, usually she informs us if she was sick but not a word was mentioned in our group text. Nick was in back-to-back trials and was getting ready to take a much-deserved vacation with his boyfriend to Mexico. Luckily, my weekend consisted of checking out new homes around Las Vegas, Henderson, and Summerlin.

Also, I desperately needed to get some much-needed sleep. Although I was working on being a bad ass bitch of taking back control of my life and finding a new freedom from the monster so he could never contact or find me again. I was tossing and turning every night not getting an ounce of sleep. By the time Friday night arrived, I crashed from exhaustion. I did not bother with dinner, I slipped into cozy pajamas and laid down drifting into a deep sleep. The morning sun rays danced across my eyes waking me. I finally gained consciousness on my whereabouts; I saw the time. *"Oh shit, I am going to be late!*" I yelled as I frantically got dressed in a hurry. I was going to be late for the house tour!

Rushing downstairs, I quickly made my way to the community that was possibly going to be called my new home. Of course, I hit every red light on the way, making me five minutes late. Thankfully the guards were kind enough to let me in without my realtor being present.

I parked outside of the house and stared in awe at it. It was beautiful, walking into the foyer and seeing the high vaulted ceilings made it feel like a mansion. Everything about this house was remarkable and the backyard with a pool was gorgeous. This was certainly an upgrade from my first home here. This house so far has won my heart over but there were three others I wanted to check out. I sat on the couch embracing the home as if it was my own. In my heart, I felt as if the home was calling me home.

We headed to the next location and the house felt cold and the guards gave off a piss off vibe. Right away I knew this house was not for me. I quickly walked through and was ready to leave. With the third house, it was cozy but nothing about this house stuck to me like the first. Before leaving, my realtor was notified that the second house and fourth house was now off the market. I was stuck with the first house and third house as my options. I pulled my agent aside and told them to put my bid in. I knew we would not hear anything until next week which is fine because my LLC would be active by then.

My text alert went off it was the group text

Tasha: Can you both come over to my house in an hour?

Nick: Sure, everything ok?

Kendra: Are you ok?

Tasha: Yes, see you soon.

I sat in my car scratching my head. Tasha has not been feeling well and she sends this cryptic text message. Something is not right. I gassed up and headed towards Tasha's place. Nick had the same feeling as I did. We pulled up at the same time 30 minutes before we were supposed to be there. *"You got a weird feeling as well?"* Nick asked. I nodded my head in agreement *"I don't know what is going on with her."* Tasha opens her door before we could ring her doorbell *"I knew you both would rush."* She mentions as she lets us in.

"Well, something is going on, you have hardly been at work and wanted to see us on the weekend out of the blue." I state. Tasha laughed as we headed towards the living room. Nick and I walked ahead of her, and he jokes in a sassy tone *"Bitch are you pregnant?"* Silence filled the room, Nick and I looked at each other before turning around to see Tasha looking down with a glowing smile as she cradles her lower stomach. A loud cheerful screech escaped my mouth ***"OH MY GOD YOU'RE PREGNANT!?"*** I excitedly jumped for joy. Nick started to cry tears of happiness *"Congratulations Tasha! You are going to be a wonderful mom!"* We all hugged each other in a group hug, excited about the unknown adventure of motherhood that Tasha is getting ready to embrace with us by her side.

We gathered around the couch to learn all the details of Tasha's growing bundle. As we sat there gossiping about the future that was going to change for the greater good. I shot up and excitedly danced around *"Can we plan your baby shower?"* Tasha sat there making us wait for her answer as she "thought" about it. She could not wipe the grin off her face as it was an easy to read *"Yes!"* Tasha nodded. Nick and I started dancing and throwing ideas out there for the theme, food, games, and so much more.

The work week has come and gone. Nick was out the door heading out for his weeklong dream vacation to Mexico. Tasha was fighting morning sickness and exhaustion. I was waiting to hear from the realtor about my bid. By the end of the day, I got a text message from the realtor.

106

Ashley: Congratulations! They accepted the bid! Make sure to send me the LLC information via email so we can get everything set up. Documents are being sent now to get your house on the market!

Kendra: Yay!!!! Thank you so much! Keeping an eye out now!

I decided to head down to my favorite coffee shop to get a celebratory chai latte and a pastry. Many things have gone great these last couple of days.

Days passed and Nick returned to work on Monday glowing from the Mexico sunrays that kissed his skin. He grabbed my hand and walked into Tasha's office where she was miserable with morning sickness. *"Guys......I am ENGAGED!"* Nick announced beaming with happiness as he showed off his stunning platinum Charles Tiffany with a 2.49 emerald cut diamond with a sweet message engraved inside "Eternal Love". Cheers of excitement echoed in Tasha's office as we congratulated Nick on his engagement. Hundreds of questions ran rapidly as we gawked over his engagement ring. Although it was all fresh and new, our excitement took over. We could not wait to start planning and celebrating.

We can hardly focus on our workload, so many exciting things are going to be happening. From a baby shower to a baby, an engagement party, and wedding. I am thrilled for the next chapters of their lives. And for me as well, I am purchasing a dream home and doing this completely anonymously because of the whole Dimitri contacting me behind bars ordeal.

I tried desperately to focus on work but by the time midafternoon came about my attention span was gone. I decided to check my emails when I heard a knock on my door. Mindy peaked her head in *"Kendra, your attorney is here."* I quickly stood up and gestured her to come in *"Come in please."* Morgan walked into my office *"Hi Kendra."* Confused by Morgan visiting, my stomach started to churn. This could not be a good sign. *"Hi Morgan, how can I help you?"* I asked. Morgan's energy was hard to read, she was a shark with her emotions shut off. I know Dimitri was put into solitary confinement for his stunt by contacting me via mail.

Morgan spoke with ease and concern *"Relax Kendra, Dimitri has gotten into massive trouble for the stunt that he pulled. I am simply visiting to see if you are considering moving and doing it anonymously so he can never find you again."* My stomach finally stopped churning from anxiety. *"Yes, I should have informed you. My LLC has been completed and I purchased a home on the other side of town in a gated and armed community. The purchase is going to take place under that LLC."* Morgan stepped back and crossed her arms with pride as she smiled *"I knew you were brilliant."*

We chatted about life and caught up on what was going on. I showed Morgan the house from the photos I took. I also informed her of Tasha's pregnancy and Nick's engagement.

Mindy knocked on my door before walking in with a bouquet of flowers. *"Kendra, the florist delivery driver dropped these off to you."* Mindy said. Confused by not knowing who sent them. I searched the bouquet to find an envelope tucked away in the wrapping. *"Someone has a secret admirer"* teased Morgan. My hands shook uncontrollably, and I gasped for air.

Kendra,

You will never get rid of me

-Dimitri